CREATION SCIENCE CLUB

The Secret Under Mystery Lake

John and Lisa Fox

The Secret Under Mystery Lake
The Creation Science Club: Book 3
by John and Lisa Fox

First printing: January 2016

ISBN 978-1-942773-02-3
Cover design: BookFuel
Design and layout: BookFuel
Style and proofreading: Dr. Robert Carter and Lita Cosner

Published by:

CREATION
BOOK PUBLISHERS

Creation Book Publishers
P.O. Box 350
Powder Springs, GA, 30127, USA.
Phone: 1-800-616-1264
creationbookpublishers.com

We dedicate this book to
Lisa's parents, Dean and Susi,
for their lives of love and service
in the name of Jesus Christ.

We also want to thank:

Buddy Davis, whose creation music ministry and dinosaur sculpting first inspired us to dig deeper into the truth,

Jonathan Sarfati, who has written books to refute the endless barrage of evolution's 'overwhelming evidence' coming at us from every side,

Creation Ministries International, for providing us all with various resources and an endless supply of 'scientific stones of truth' for our slings.

With special gratitude to Dr. Robert Carter, Lita Cosner, and others at CMI for taking the time to review this book.

*Note: If any errors or misuse of terms or facts occur in this series, these mistakes are solely the responsibility of the authors.

CHAPTER 1

"Aaron! Hey, Aaron, wait up!" David and Jack caught up to their new friend in the school hallway. They each grabbed one of his arms, turned him around, and started forcefully directing him toward room 202.

"Man, there ain't no escape," David said.

"You know we need you on our team," Jack added.

Aaron was a good deal taller than both David and Jack, especially David. And, although he was pretty lean, he could have whipped either of his friends before the tardy bell rang. However, he only half-resisted as they slid him into the school counselor's office.

A fifty-something-year-old woman wearing bifocals looked up and smiled as the boys scuffled into her office. "Well, well, Mr. Franklin, it looks like your friends want you to talk to me about something."

Aaron Franklin blushed a bit. "Uh, yeah…I guess they want you to put me into their honors science class."

Ten minutes later, the boys were outside in the school yard playing keep-away with Aaron's jacket all tied up into a ball. Laughing and joking around, they didn't notice the red-headed boy watching them until their jacket ball landed near his feet.

"Hey, Todd!" David called to the boy. "Ya wanna play?"

Mixed emotions crossed over Todd's face. He looked down at the jacket at his feet, then up at the smiling boys in front of him. He took a step toward them, then stopped.

"Come on," Jack called. "We can play four-man keep-away."

Todd looked at Aaron, then looked down at the ground. Clenching his fists, he kicked the jacket ball right into a puddle of muddy water.

"Hey, Man!" Aaron yelled. "Whatcha doin'?"

Todd turned on his heels as he yelled back, "My Pa says if we just ignore your kind, maybe you'll go back to the East Side where you belong!" Then he ran off without looking back.

The fun was instantly over and the three friends just stood there for a few seconds. Then, Aaron angrily kicked his jacket out of the mud and sat on the ground without looking at Jack or David. "I knew we shouldn't have moved here! It's called *Greenville*, but they might as well call it *Whiteville*." Glancing up at Todd's retreating figure, Aaron sighed. "People around here act like I've got some kinda disease."

While Jack untied Aaron's jacket and shook off the dirty water, David reached out a hand to help his friend up. "Yeah, man," David said, "you're right. Greenville is just about as white as it gets. But, I guess they can't help it. If *white* is all they've ever known, it's gonna take them a while to get used to some *color*. I mean, you wouldn't believe how many times I've been called *Chico* or *Paco*—and I've lived here practically my whole life."

"You know," Jack said, "you're black, David's Latino, and I'm white…but, on the inside we're all the same. Red, brown, yellow, black, or white—it doesn't matter—we're all part of the same family. It says so right in the Bible."

"In the Bible?" Aaron looked surprised. "Wow! I didn't know that."

David laughed and slapped Aaron on the shoulder. "I'm a-thinkin' there's a couple friends of mine that you need to be meetin'."

* * * * * * *

As David and Aaron hopped out of the van, David's mom reminded them, "I'll be at the end of the lane around 6:00 to get you."

"Yeah, Mama. Thanks a lot," David called as the van pulled away.

While the boys walked through the melting slush on the long winding lane, Aaron told David, "Man, I just can't get over it. Back in Jersey, we liked to visit the Metro Park. But, around here…it's like everyone lives in their very own *personal* park."

David laughed. "Yep. Around here folks like their own space." Looking around at the acres of trees just starting to bud, David shook his head. "I can't imagine living right in the middle of street after street of houses all packed together. Didn't you feel like everyone was looking in your windows and listening to everything you were saying?"

"Naw," Aaron shrugged. "It's not like that. People mostly keep to themselves, unless there's trouble. Then help's only a shout away. Ya know, the city has its good points."

"That's true, I guess…" David said without sounding convinced. Then, pointing up the lane, he announced, "There's Billy's place. They call it *ErinWood.* I guess that's what it's been called for more than 100 years."

Billy's place was a beautifully restored log cabin, complete with a front porch that seemed to speak the words, *Come on and sit down—kick up your feet and we'll talk a while.*

"Ain't no name better than *AaronWood*," Aaron beamed.

David snickered. "Sorry, man, but it's *Erin* as in *E-r-i-n*. It's a girl's name."

Before Aaron could respond, two mixed mutts and a cat had come running over to meet them. The dogs barked and wagged excitedly at David's greeting, then sat politely to be introduced to Aaron. A woman with dark wavy hair and a glint of mischief in her eyes called from off the porch, "Hey, David! Billy and the T-twins are out in the work shed. You tell 'em cookies will be out in 20 minutes."

As the two headed back toward a large shed, David explained, "That's Mrs. Carmen James, but we all just call her Mrs. Carmen. She's as sweet as apple pie, and nobody—I mean nobody—makes better cookies than she does."

Walking into the work shed, Aaron's eyes took a minute to adjust to the dimmer lighting. Then, he gasped, "Whoa! Like, are those dinosaurs?"

David laughed at his friend's surprise. "Aren't they totally cool? I purposely didn't tell you. Billy and the Tadue twins have been working on some dinosaur sculptures for a couple of the showcases in Dr. Ted's museum."

"Well, if they made these, they sure are good," Aaron said as he walked around. "Look, here's a *Psittacosaurus*. Whoa, over here is a nest full of babies—looks like they're *Maiasaura*." Reaching out a finger, he started to touch one of the babies. "They almost seem real…"

The mother *Maiasaura* whipped her head around to face Aaron. Opening her mouth right in front of his face, she let out a loud, shrieking, "*Hah-issss…*" It was a hair-raising sound.

Aaron shot two feet straight up off the ground, then turned 180 degrees and started running even before he had landed. And out the door he shot like a rocket. But when the sounds of laughter caught up with him, he stopped, turned around, and jogged sheepishly back toward the shed. "Those were, like, totally freak-out realistic!"

"Whoa, Aaron-dude!" Darin shook his head in amazement. "David told us that you were a born athlete, but he didn't tell us you were Michael Jordan and LeBron James rolled into one!"

David wiped the tears out of his eyes. "Sorry, man. I guess I 'forgot' to tell you that the dinos are animatronic."

****

After eating every last crumb of Mrs. James' two dozen monster-sized cookies, along with a big ol' pitcher of milk, everyone gathered out on the front porch to enjoy the early spring thaw. The breeze was warm and balmy…so nice.

"Well, Aaron," Billy said with his typical fun-loving smile, "now that you've met us, I hope you'll hang around enough to get to know us. If you think you'd be interested, we're planning on having a big *Spring Break Camp Out* right here at ErinWood. We'd love to have you."

"Sounds fantastic!" Aaron said enthusiastically, then added, "Would it be okay if I brought my sister, Tasha, along? She's in the eleventh grade—a real brain. I guess she hasn't made many friends, yet."

"Of course, she can come. Tell you what—why don't you leave your number, and Carmen and I will give your folks a call. If they're okay with it, maybe the two of you can ride on over with David and the Hill twins to help get things set up over the next couple of weeks. There's lots to do, and we can use all the help we can get."

Mrs. Carmen handed Aaron a piece of paper and a pencil, and he wrote down his parents' names and phone number. "How many kids are coming to the camp out?"

"We're thinking five or so boys and the same number of girls…enough to be fun, but not so many as to be out of control. Of course, there'll be other adults besides just Carmen and me. And, we'll have some help from a family we made friends with down in Argentina."

"That's right," David laughed, "a family of *dino-Soures*."

"Dinosaurs? Yeah, right." Aaron shook his head.

From down the lane, everyone heard two long horn blasts. "Come on," David called as he jumped off the porch. "I'll explain about the Soure family in the van." Everyone waved and shouted goodbye.

Darin sighed and said dreamily, "Rebekah is my very favoritest kind of dinosaur."

Abel grunted in disgust, but then jumped up. "Look, it's the spring's first morning cloak."

As Darin and Abel took off after the butterfly, Billy put his arm around his wife. "David tells me that some of the kids at school have a problem with the color of Aaron's skin." After a pause, he continued, "I think the Lord's putting a new twist into the theme of our *Spring Break Camp Out*."

CHAPTER 2

As the wind whistled past his ears, 14-year-old Andru Sanders wished he could somehow go just ten seconds back in time. Surely, he would have made a different decision. Standing up on the ledge with his little sister and younger cousins, he had felt indestructible. But now, he was sure he would die. He had smiled, bowed grandly, and made the leap. What had he been thinking? He felt like he had been falling for miles!

Splash! Down he went into the cool dim depths of the lake. Down…down…he just kept going down. As soon as he could, he brought himself to a stop. *Out!* All he wanted was out. As he stroked upward, he made a mental promise to never show off again.

But then, not more than a foot away, he saw something looking directly at him. It was a long, lean boy. They stared at each other for only a brief moment, then the mysterious boy arced and dived down—down into the darkness of the lake. Dru's lungs urged him to go up, and fast! So, he reached for the growing light above him.

Breaking through into the sunshine, Dru gasped for air, then waited for the other boy to surface. But no one came up. Spinning around, he strained to see where the boy might be.

Looking up toward his friends, he called out, "Where is he?"

"Where's who?" his 13-year-old cousin, Ana, called back.

Dru continued treading water, looking in every direction. "The boy," he shouted, starting to panic. "Where's the boy who was with me in the water?"

"Dru," his sister Christy answered, "what are you talking about? We're the only ones here. Come out now!"

But, without another word, Dru dived back under the water. Swimming down, he strained his eyes through the dimness for a glimpse of the boy. Nothing! Surfacing again for a quick breath, he dived once more. "I saw him," he thought to himself, "I know it. Was he hurt? Could I have helped him?"

Coming up for another breath, Dru was ready to dive again, but his cousin Josiás yelled, "Dru, stop! What's wrong? Are you okay?"

Dru paused. Was he okay? It just didn't make sense. How could that boy have gotten into the lake without them seeing him? And why would he purposely swim down instead of up?

Now Christy called, "Dru, come out! You're scaring me!"

Dru looked blankly up at his little sister and cousins. They had come down to a lower ledge now. They all looked worried. But Dru couldn't give up his search. He had to help the boy. He yelled to his friends, "I'm okay." Then, he dived once more, going as deep as he could. He thought he saw what seemed to be dim lights below him, but he just couldn't see far enough.

Suddenly, he saw a hand reach out from above him. Long fingers wrapped around his wrist like a vice and began pulling him. Fear ripped through his body. Up to this point he had been scared for the missing boy. Now he was scared for himself. He began to fight. He twisted and tried to pull away. But the hand held him tight. His heart beat fast and his lungs screamed for air. He began to feel dizzy, then suddenly he was breaking out into the hot spring sun.

"Are you crazy!" Ana yelled at him. "What's wrong with you? You're making Christy cry! And I'm gonna tell Uncle Christopher if you don't get out of the water right now!"

In a bit of a daze, Dru realized it had been Ana who had grabbed him. She had been trying to pull him back up. Dru watched Ana swim back toward the rocks where she could climb out. Feeling weak and uncertain, Dru slowly followed her back toward solid ground. Was he okay? Was he crazy? Had he really seen anyone down there?

Josiás, Ana's 12-year-old brother, was waiting by the shore to help Dru out of the water. "Man, Dru, I'm sure glad you're okay."

Once Dru sat down, Christy ran to sit down beside him. She knew he wouldn't want her to hug him, but she just needed to be close to him. "Dru, why did you keep going down like that? What were you looking for?"

But, before Dru could answer, Ana, who had her back turned angrily toward Dru, swung around just long enough to say, "He was looking for his brains. Obviously, he bashed 'em out when he hit the water." She turned back away, but then threw over her shoulder, "That is—if he had any brains to begin with."

"Give it up, Ana!" Josiás said to his sister. "We were all scared. Look, even Dru's shook up. Let's just forget about it and go home."

Before they got home, Dru made peace with Ana. "Hey, I'm sorry I scared you guys. I didn't mean to. It's just that…I saw someone…well, I thought I saw something down there. Anyway," he continued, "thanks for helping me and all."

All the anger left Ana immediately. "Man, Dru, I'm just glad you're okay. I mean, we've been dreaming about moving here for two years. It wouldn't be good to get killed in the first week, would it?" Then she added, "What were you looking for, anyway?"

Even as he started to answer, Dru could see the long, lean boy beneath the lake's surface—his blond hair and striped shirt. He shivered at the thought. Was the boy okay? Was there even a boy at all? "Well..." Dru hesitated, "it must have just been some big, strange-looking fish, or something, I guess."

That night on his bed, Dru looked out toward Rocky Reach—the slender finger of Mystery Lake that curved its way onto the Sanders' new property. Again, Dru saw the face of the mysterious boy in the lake. Quietly to himself, he said, "He didn't look hurt. He *did* look afraid, but not of drowning. He looked afraid of...well, of me. Then he dived down—down like a fish. It just doesn't make sense."

Then, he thought about Ana's angry words: "He was looking for his brains. Obviously, he bashed 'em out when he hit the water." Maybe she was right. Maybe he had hit his head. Maybe he had blacked out for a second. Maybe it had all been some kind of a dream or something. Yeah, that was the only thing that made any sense...just a dream. Boy, would Mom ever worry if she knew he'd been dumb enough to knock himself out in the water. And, man, Dad would be sure to say no more swimming without adult supervision. So, Dru decided to just keep quiet. Yeah, he'd best just forget all about it and try to get to sleep.

****

While Andru tossed about unable to sleep, another boy also lay awake. Thirteen-year-old Enoch Dickens reached down to scoop up the soft ball of a kitten that was mewing for his attention. Snuggling his pet close, Eno dangled his leg down to the cave floor, swinging his hammock slowly to and fro as he considered what he had done and what he had seen.

Enoch was what his people called a *strapper.* He was beyond boyhood, but had not yet reached manhood. As only a strapper, he was prohibited from approaching within twenty feet of the surface of the lake. Eno had never known a strapper to break this rule. He himself had never planned to break it. But, today had been just so…well, so…hard. He buried his face into little Leah's purring side and tried to remember his mother's words: "Love your enemies. Forgive those who hurt you." It seemed too hard, but he knew the words were straight from the Holy Book—so it must be the will of the Maker.

Then, Eno's conscience pricked him. The Holy Book also said he should obey the given rules. But, he had purposely swam up—up toward the light that came from the burning sun. Even when he saw the clear twenty-foot markers, he had kept going up. But…would not the Loving Creator understand? Mrs. Bethany said that God was the one who had put this longing in him in the first place. But…she had also said that he must wait for God's time, that he must not run ahead of the Lord.

But…but…what a rotten day it had been. Earlier in the day, after he had accidentally dropped his net of weeds in the field, Ben had called him a *scrawny half-sized pike.* Then, later, when all the other strappers were done with their field chores, Eno had still been working to finish up. His friend Miriam had come to help him. Then, at the East Entrance Cavern, James had been waiting for them—waiting just to sneer: "Only a sun-bleached American would need the help of a maiden." It seemed everyone could work harder and longer than he could. Even his little brother, Jacob—hardly more than a small-fry—could outdistance him.

Then later, off sulking by himself, Enoch had looked up toward the surface of the lake. What was it like up there—up under nothing? It seemed that every dream he had ever dreamed had centered on the land above him, the land he knew he would never see. Or would he? So, he was nothing but a *scrawny half-sized pike*, was he? Nothing but a *sun-bleached American*? Well, he would show them! Shooting away from the breathing bubble, he had stroked with all his might toward the shimmering surface of the lake above him.

Breaking through the barrier that only a few scouts had ever broken, Enoch had felt a warmth that was brand new to him. The sun hurt his eyes badly, but the air was delicious to breath—so dry and light. Hiding from the bright sun, Eno had swam in the sun-warmed waters just below the surface of the lake. It was a marvelous place to be. He felt so warm and light—all the pressure of the depths was gone. He felt he could swim with the ease of a trout.

Fifteen forbidden minutes had gone by when he had decided he had better head back down before he was caught. But, when he had surfaced for a last sun-warmed breath, he heard voices above the lake. Fear shot through him as he realized there must be Americans close by. What if they saw him? What if they took him prisoner or enslaved him?

Then, through the glaring light, Eno had seen a figure jumping right toward where he was. Without making a ripple, Eno had disappeared below the waters and began swimming for the bottom. But then, like an arrow, the American had shot past him. Eno had pulled back but, suddenly, they were face to face. After locking eyes with the land-lover for a brief moment, Enoch had arched and dived down, while the American had swam up toward the blazing sun.

Back near the bottom of Emerald Lake, regret had filled Enoch's thoughts. What would the Elders do if they knew he had broken through the surface? Surely he would be punished. And, how disappointed Mrs. Bethany would be. Dear, kind, old Mrs. Bethany…and, his parents…oh, my!

Now, lying in his hammock, Eno whispered to his kitten, "Leah, I saw an American land-lover today. His hair and skin were bleached, just like mine. His eyes were faded and pale, just like mine. And, I am sure by his face that he was no older than I…" Eno stared for a long time at the small light in his rocky cove. Pictures, thoughts, and feelings all swam through his mind, until his eyelids began to get heavy. He put Leah down to go to her mama. Then, swaying back and forth, his last thoughts were, "I have to go back up. The sun is calling me. The air, the sky, even the American strapper, they are all calling me. I just have to see it all again."

****

Out around the campfire by the ErinWood fishing pond, everyone leaned forward, eagerly waiting to hear what would happen next. But, Billy just smiled, leaned back against his tree stump, and said, "That's it for tonight."

"No way!" several voices complained.

"Does Andru tell anybody what he saw?"

"And what about Enoch? Is he from Atlantis or something?"

"Sorry," Billy laughed. "Don't worry, I'll tell more of the story in the morning. But for now, Darin and Rebekah have got a great night hike all planned out."

CHAPTER 3

Sitting down at her assigned desk, Ana Garcia looked shyly around the seventh-grade classroom. Fourteen other kids sat around her, all whispering curiously about the 'new girl.' Ana wished she were back in Huron. There, the classes had been big enough to hide in. And the kids at Ana's old school had come from all kinds of different ethnic backgrounds. So, she hadn't stuck out like pepper in the salt, like she did here. Some had been black and some white, there had been Asians and Latinos, and there had been all sorts of multi-racial mixes—like Ana. Ana's mom was white. Her dad, on the other hand, was Latin American. And *his* dad had been a Caribbean black. Ana carried a lot of her grandfather's looks.

Ana was a lovely girl, full of energy, with a bit of a temper. She enjoyed sports and laughing with friends. Up to this point in her life, she had never had any reason to feel out of place or unaccepted. But now, here she was—two states down and two states over—out in the middle of nowhere—small-town U.S.A. Here, everything was going to be different. Looking around her, Ana saw nothing but white faces and freckles.

Two doors down, 12-year-old Josiás sat in the sixth grade classroom. He smiled bravely at the curious faces around him. Most of the kids smiled back. But a couple of bigger boys scowled at him. Joe thought everyone looked strange. In Huron, he had been used to real diversity—Afro hair, Asian eyes, European noses, and everything in between. (Joe himself was lighter than his sister, with more Latino features.) But, here, everyone seemed to look alike. They even dressed the same—tight-fitting jeans and t-shirts of various colors.

"Young man? Um, Chico…?" the teacher's voice called out politely.

Joe saw that she was looking directly at him, so, blushing, he responded, "Yes, m'am?"

"Please come here," she said, motioning with her hand.

Josiás stood up and walked between the aisles toward the teacher's desk. One of the girls smiled encouragingly at him. But one of the scowling boys whispered in a mocking tone as he passed, "Chico—Chico-Bambito." Joe felt himself blushing again. His father had warned him that their family would stand out in their new town. He had been prepared for people to stare at him. But, he hadn't expected people to be mean to him for no reason.

As he reached the front of the room, Mrs. Evans spoke to him with loud, over-enunciated words. "You - need - to - write - your - name - here…Do - you - understand?"

Joe sighed and tried to smile. He knew she was really trying to be kind. "It's okay, Mrs. Evans," he answered. "I grew up speaking English."

Mrs. Evans looked both embarrassed and relieved. "Oh…I'm glad. That will make things easier. Now, could you please tell me how to pronounce your name? Is it *Josie-us*?"

The two big boys in the front row snickered and whispered, "Josie-wosie!" Joe sighed again, then told Mrs. Evans, "It's okay, you can just call me *Joe*." He knew it was going to be a long first day.

****

When the school day did finally end, Dru and Christy met Ana and Joe outside by the school parking lot. They were all glad to see each other. Christy ran over to Ana and hugged her excitedly. "I made three new friends already. They invited me to eat at their lunch table."

Ana smiled at Christy, glad to be back with someone who wasn't afraid to touch her. Nobody had actually been mean to Ana. People had smiled and all—but, they had kind of treated her like she was from a different planet, not just a different state.

Dru was glad to hear his sister had gotten along well. He always felt a bit extra protective of her since she was so small for her age. Looking at Joe, he asked, "How was the sixth grade class? Make any new friends?"

Joe tried to act more positive than he felt. "Yeah, man," he said. "A couple of nice girls showed me around." He didn't mention the *Chico-Bambito* incident, or the fact that one of the girls had asked him what it was like to live in Mexico. Joe had never been out of the United States.

"Well," Ana said with a smile, "at least the school year's almost over. One more month and we'll have the whole summer to do nothing but explore 200 acres of beautiful countryside." Then, she added with a sigh, "I guess that'll make coming into a tiny little all-white school worth it."

Christy looked into her cousin's face and began to realize that Ana's day hadn't been as easy as hers had been. Looking at Joe, she could see the same strain. Dru must have sensed it, too, because he said, "Don't worry guys. In a day or two, everyone will see you're regular people, just like the rest of us."

Before they had time to talk more, Ana and Joe's mom, Abigail Garcia, pulled up in their red van. The cousins all piled in and started chattering about fixing up the old stable on the Garcias' land. When the decision to move had been made, Mr. Tomás Garcia had promised his older two children each a pony. And, the Sanders family had decided to help fix up the Garcias' stable before working on building one on their own land.

It was a pretty long trek home along some pretty narrow country roads, but no one in the van minded. They were driving toward a dream-come-true. Years of hoping, planning, and working had all come together when a family at church had told Tomás about their grandpa having some land for sale. Yes, land and space and endless adventure was waiting for them at the end of this bumpy gravel road leading toward Mystery Lake.

****

Gliding through the water, Enoch moved along Finney Tunnel until he felt the familiar pattern that belonged to Miriam's home. Ducking down, he swerved to the right, then up into a small area where the tunnel roof had been chipped out to create a comfortably-sized breathing space.

Once Eno caught his breath, he struck the bell located near the small fish-oil lamp. Within a few seconds, a deeper bell answered his, telling him he was welcome to enter. Diving down, he swam easily through the 15-foot entrance tunnel to the BearClaw family home.

Swimming up into the parlor room, he pulled himself out of the water and greeted Mrs. Bethany BearClaw, who sat in a padded chair near the brightest light in the room. Five or six small birds twittered around her head, eager for the treats she held in her hand.

Next to his own mother and father, Eno felt closer to Mrs. Bethany than to any other adult in all of Eden. She was very kind, wise with her words, and always seemed to know just what Enoch needed to hear. And perhaps just as importantly, she was the only other Edenite who had light skin, light hair, and light eyes, just like he did.

"Ah, Master Enoch," Mrs. Bethany said with a smile, "it is always good to see you. But, I am afraid Miss Miriam will not be able to go out with you this afternoon. She must watch the small-fry while her mother preserves all the peeka fruit Mr. Gideon is bringing in from the fields." Then she asked, "Are you not needed in helping your father to harvest your family's peeka?"

"No, m'am," Enoch answered. "Father plans to begin harvest the day after tomorrow. Actually, I was hoping Mimi could go to Sunshine Caverns with me one more time before the busy summer days in the fields began. But," he added in a dejected tone, "I guess they have already begun."

Mrs. Bethany didn't ask Eno why he didn't go to Sunshine Caverns with another friend. She knew that the other boys his age didn't like to do much with Enoch. It just seemed hard for them to accept someone so obviously different. The girls treated him better, but, besides Miriam, they were either too young or too old to make good playmates for him.

"Well, then," Mrs. Bethany said with a determined tone, "I guess I will just have to go to the caverns with you."

Enoch wasn't so sure going to the caverns with Mrs. Bethany would be much fun since she was nearly 70. However, he wouldn't have hurt her feelings for the world. So, he said, "Really, Mrs. Bethany? That would be great!" Then, after telling the BearClaw family of their plans, the two friends slipped into the water and followed the tunnels out to Sunshine Caverns.

At the caverns, they swam in the extra warm waters and even climbed some of the lower rocks and ledges. While Mrs. Bethany rested on a large ledge, Enoch climbed all the way to Sunshine Plateau, where, for a few short hours during the long summer days, the sun found its way down into the Edenites' underground world. Enoch stood in the receding sunbeam. It didn't seem to be able to carry its warmth all the way to him. Instead, it was like a vision calling him to follow it up, up, up to the land where it reigned as king of the sky.

Coming back down to sit with Mrs. Bethany, Enoch hugged his knees while she remembered the good old days of her youth. Eno smiled and said, "I cannot picture you being a strapper, Mrs. Bethany."

She laughed and reminded him primly, "In those days, girls were referred to as *maidens*. A gentleman would have never called a girl a *strapper*. My, how times have changed," she added thoughtfully. "In those days, there had still been plenty of food to harvest from the lake floor. Gardens were only grown for luxury foods. Bethel was just being chipped out. And, in those days, there had been at least a dozen, maybe more, *blond* Edenites. Of course, these days, they call us *sun-bleached*."

"Mrs. Bethany," Eno interrupted, "if the founders of Eden were sun-bleached, why do all the strappers look down on my light hair and skin?"

Mrs. Bethany understood his questions. "Dear Master Enoch, before you were born, it had been decades since a blond Edenite was born. It is natural for people to feel uncomfortable around someone who is different. Some, however, follow the Savior's example and look past the outside and honor what is on the inside. But," she continued, "many people have trouble looking beyond the outside. When this happens, even good people can make bad choices."

Hugging his knees tightly, Eno suddenly burst out, "Mrs. Bethany, do you not ever long to live in the land of the sun—where the air is so warm and light? Where there is nothing above your head? Where the colors are so bright that they hurt your eyes?"

Mrs. Bethany reached over and touched his hand. "Enoch, I too have felt the longing you now feel." Then she looked into his face and told him, "Since the day I first saw you, I knew you were special. I felt like the Maker had given me a son to replace the two I had lost. And, I believe that God, your Maker, has a special plan for you. But," she said, "as I have warned you before—you must be careful to follow God's leading. Do not be rash or you might put all of Eden in danger."

Enoch wondered if he should tell Mrs. Bethany that he had already been rash—that, in his frustration, he had gone to the forbidden surface of the lake, that he had seen and been seen by an American boy. He decided not to say anything. However, he didn't realize that Mrs. Bethany could read his face, and she had already guessed the truth.

****

Enoch left Mrs. Bethany back at the BearClaw cave and then started home feeling special. Mrs. Bethany's words were running over and over again in his mind: "I have prayed for you...God has a special plan for you...Follow God..." But, then, everything was spoiled. Enoch paused, just for a breath, in the town green. He was ready to continue home when James and one of the older strappers called out in a mocking voice, "Hey, Enoch! Did old Mrs. Bethany out-swim you to the Caverns?"

All of Enoch's joy drained out of his heart. But, he tried to remember his father's words to *turn the other cheek*. So, he merely answered, "We had a good time. Mrs. Bethany is very kind."

"I am sure she is to *you*," James said. "And we all know why, too!"

"Yeah!" the older boy said. "We know why she thinks you are so special."

Enoch was surprised. "You do?"

James looked around to make sure that no one else was listening. Then he said, "Sure we do. Come here and we will tell you."

Eno swam over and pulled himself up by the boys. "It is like this," James began. "Mrs. Bethany used to live by the hot springs that bubble up into the sun dwellers' land of America. Well, I have heard that folks there could hardly keep Mrs. Bethany down in Eden. They say she had an endless longing for the land of the blazing sun, said she could not help it, said it came with her bleached hair and skin.

"Well, one time—not long after the death of her second son, Mrs. Bethany was well over fifty at that time—she disappeared. All of Eden searched for her, but no one could find her. Then, suddenly, she reappeared, just showed up back home like she had gone to the library or something." James stopped and leaned toward Enoch and said, "Guess what happened the next day."

Enoch wished he could tell James to grow up, and that he did not care what he said. But, instead he whispered, "What happened?"

James laughed. "Can you believe it? He has never guessed the truth in all these years."

Eno was so frustrated he clenched his hands. But, he made himself speak calmly, and simply asked again, "Tell me, what happened?"

James continued, "The next day, the very next day, your father and mother announced the birth of their firstborn—a son—*you*."

Enoch felt let down. "So?" he asked. "What does my being born have to do with what you were saying?"

James rolled his eyes. "You are as slow at thinking as you are at swimming! Do you not get it? Mrs. Bethany went up to America and stole some sun-bleached American's baby and brought it down here to replace her son. So, you see, you are not really an Edenite after all. You are just some poor American's baby that Mrs. Bethany brought down here and gave to your parents to raise for her."

Enoch felt so shocked that he just stared at James and the other boy. His mind began to whirl with all sorts of questions: maybe that was why he was so light…maybe that was why he longed so for the land of the sun…maybe that was why he looked so different from his little sister and brother…maybe that was why Mrs. Bethany treated him so special…

But then, a loud laugh pulled Eno back to the strappers in front of him. James was saying, "I told you, I told you he would believe it. He is so gullible, he would believe anything."

Eno didn't wait to hear more. He pushed himself back into the water and swam as fast as he could until he reached his home cavern. Once there, he ran to find his mother. She listened—listened to his anger, his frustration, and his hurt. And, in her face, he could see sympathy and understanding. But, her only words were: "Do not let hate or ugliness grow up in you, my son. Pray for the help of God to love. It is the command of the Lord Jesus, 'You must love one another.' Remember, love will always win."

Then, Eno's little brother, Jacob, came running over to him. He excitedly told him that he had found a hidden bird's nest among the various plants they grew along the cavern walls. Eno reached down and touched Jacob's one-sided dimple. Then, he reached up and touched his own one-sided dimple. And, in his mind, he could see the same dimple on his father's cheek. He felt comforted that God had made sure that he had inherited his father's dimple. And, somehow, knowing God's personal love for him helped him to forgive James for his unkind words. His mother had been right, love was helping him win.

****

Ten silent teenagers sat absolutely still—trying not to break the spell. But Billy was merciless. "That's it for this morning," he said with a chuckle. Then, standing up, he told them, "You'll just have time to help Mrs. James and Mrs. Soure clean up the breakfast things before Mr. Avila leads us in devotions. Then, Abel and Stego have set up a treasure hunt."

As the kids jumped up to get to work, Aaron and Jack stayed to ask Billy a question.

"Hey, Billy," Jack began, "Aaron and I were talking. We both know about Adam and Eve from Sunday school. And, we know they were the first people ever and that they were fully human and all. But…well, I mean…"

Aaron spoke up, "Well, if Adam and Eve were white, then where did black folks come from? And, if Adam and Eve were black, then where did white folks come from?"

"And," Jack jumped back in, "if Adam was black and Eve was white, then where did Asian people come from, or Native Americans, or Hispanics?"

Billy smiled and waved for the boys to follow him up to the cabin. "You know, guys, that's a really common question." Rubbing his chin, he said, "You see, when God made the first man and woman, He created them with all sorts of hidden genetic information and potential for change."

"Like hidden information to make black or white skin," Aaron supposed.

"Well, actually," Billy responded, "white, or light-colored skin, comes from a mutation that…"

"So, I'm a mutant?" Jack pondered.

Billy chuckled. "Well, in a way, yes. You see, there's a mutation found in folks of European descent that reduces the amount of melanin that reaches the surface of their skin."

"So, more melanin reaching the surface of my skin is what makes my skin dark?" Aaron asked.

"Exactly," Billy answered.

"So, it's not just hidden genetic information, but also certain mutations that have caused all the diversity we see in different people," Jack stated.

"You got it, mutant-boy," Billy nodded. "God has used these ways to create all the colors of skin, eye colors, hair colors, and texture…"

"Big noses, unibrows, and flat feet…" Aaron added.

Billy laughed, "Yep, I think you guys get it."

Passing by the work shed, Billy paused to explain, "In Genesis, it makes it all pretty clear how different people groups formed. As the population grew after Noah's Flood, the people all stayed together. But, their attitudes and lives did not please God, and He decided it would be better to separate them. So, He confused their languages. Well, each group of people that spoke a common language went off to a different place to live together. So, different people groups grew up."

"Hey," Jack said excitedly, "that was the Tower of Babel."

"You got it!" Billy said. "Anyway, as the genes of each separate group mixed, different genes were more dominant or, in some cases (according to where the people lived), certain genes were more successful. So, over time," he summarized, "different people groups became more and more defined."

As the three of them approached the rented shelter the campers were using for meals, David called over to his friends, "Whatchu lazy bums doing? We're already done here. I guess you two get to haul the garbage down to the end of the lane."

Billy slapped the boys on the back and said, "You know what? Dr. Veritas and Dr. Lution plan to cover all these kinds of issues at their new Creation Museum. It will be great for everyone to get a better understanding of how it all works." Then he pushed the boys toward the trash bags David was holding out to them. "Now, go get to it!" he laughed.

CHAPTER 4

Dru stood up and looked with interest at the hill that rose up behind the Community Church Camp Grounds. Since the youth leaders had given the group two hours of free time, Dru turned to Joe and said, "Hey, let's go check out that hill. It looks like it's got a big bite taken out of it or something."

After a good hike, Dru and Joe found themselves about halfway up the hill, standing at the bottom edge of a gigantic hole.

"How cool!" Joe said looking around him. "This isn't just a hole. It's like a crater."

Dru agreed. "Something must have blown a hole in the side of this hill. But you can tell it was a long time ago, since it's all grown in with brush and trees now."

"I heard that some gold diggers blew up a bunch of old dynamite here—long time ago," Joe said.

"Ah, that ain't nothing but a sissy cover-up, Chico-Bambito," a voice said from behind some brush. Looking through the dimming light, the two boys saw two other boys walking toward them. It was Trent and Brent, the two cousins from Joe's class. They were big boys, already 14, but had been held back since they seemed more interested in causing trouble than in learning their lessons.

"Hey, Dru-boy!" Brent said in an insulting tone. "I bet you and Chico haven't heard the *real* story behind this here crater."

"No, Brent," Trent said with mock fear, "don't tell it. Little Josie-wosie will have to hold his mama's hand to go to sleep tonight. You know they live right by Rocky Ridge—right where those…those *things* live."

The hairs on the back of Dru's neck began to bristle. He could remember so clearly the long, lean boy under the water. Had Trent and Brent also seen something strange in the lake? Trying to sound nonchalant, Dru said, "No, man. We haven't heard the story. But if you'd like to tell it, we'll listen."

Trent rubbed his hands together with a glint in his eyes. Then he sat down on a big stone. "Well, don't you forget now that y'all asked for it," he said. Then, in a hushed, mysterious voice he began, "More than a hundred years ago, Hill Valley weren't even a town. The only thing even on any map was Mystery Lake. And, it weren't called *Mystery Lake* then, neither. It was just plain ol' *Emerald Lake*. Y'all know that's its real name still. But, nobody 'round here calls it that. And, I'll tell you why.

"Before people had much even settled around these parts, just the explorers and fortune seekers came through. Well, one night, close to midnight, a group of three horsemen were cuttin' their way back east past ol' Emerald Lake. As they rode along, suddenly a bright shootin' star came fallin' to earth. In disbelief, the horsemen watched as the star came closer and closer; then, with a giant explosion, it buried itself right into the side of this here hill. Right here, right where we're sittin'."

Everyone took a moment to look around. It was nearly dark now. Then, Trent continued, "Course, those three men were brave as bears and knew that there ain't been nobody that'd seen a shootin' star land. So, they rode their horses up the hill, up above where the star had hit. Dirt and rocks and all sorts of mess had flown everywhere. Then, down there in the center of the crater was a smallish sort of thing all lit up. Those men could tell right off that it weren't no star. No, sir! It had shafts of light comin' out from several perfectly square doorways.

"In amazement, the men watched as these strange sort of creatures slid out of the doorways. They were long, slimy creatures—lookin' a bit like people, but they didn't walk. No, they slipped and slid and slimed their way down the hillside in the darkness of the night.

"Now, though them men were brave as bears, they were smart ones, too. They weren't fool enough to go near creatures from some different planet. So, they just sort of followed the aliens' slimy trail from a distance. All night, they slowly followed. Then, just before dawn, they had reached the edge of Emerald Lake, right there by Rocky Ridge, right there by where you live now," he added, looking right at Dru and Joe.

Again, the boys were quiet. Joe was about to laugh off the creepy feeling that was building up in him, but Dru interrupted with growing interest. "So, what happened next?"

"Brent will tell the rest of the story," Trent answered. "After all, his grandpa, he's seen 'em with his own eyes. Hasn't he, Brent?"

"That's right, he sure 'nough has," Brent replied. "And my grandpa, he's as honest as old Abe Lincoln himself. You can ask anyone."

So, Brent continued with the story. "You can bet those horsemen traveled a good five miles off from the lake before they bedded down for a few hours of sleep. But then, the next day, when the sun was high in the sky, they rode down to ol' Emerald Lake. For some reason, as they got closer, say 40 feet from the shore, the horses wouldn't go no closer.

"Now, these weren't no scaredy, nervous horses, neither. But, like Trent, here, said, those three men were brave as bears and born explorers. So, they climbed down off their horses and followed that smooth trail them creatures had left leadin' right up to the lake.

"Well, standin' there a-scratchin' their heads, the men were thinkin', *What in the world*, when, suddenly, about 20 feet away, the fish started just a-jumpin' right up out of the water. Maybe ten fish, big and small, just jumped right up into the air. One even landed on the shore.

"Two of the horsemen ran right over to see what was happenin'. Then, seemingly out of nowhere, two long slimy hands reached up and grabbed a booted foot of each of the men. Quicker than they could yell, they was gone. Down they went. Never did come back up, neither—never."

"Oh, wow, man!" Joe said in a nervous tone. "What happened to the other guy, the third horseman?"

Trent shrugged his shoulders, and said, "Well, he got away. That's how we know the story. He took his friends' horses and rode like the wind outta there. And then, at the first town he came to, he told everyone what had happened. At first, no one believed him. They all thought, you know, maybe the guy just sort of got rid of the other two so that he could...umm, keep their goods. So, the sheriff put him in jail, and took some other men and rode on out to Emerald Lake.

"When they got here, they found everything almost just as the man had said—the hole in the hill, the smoothed trail close to the lake, even some of the two missin' men's boot tracks by the lake. They never did find them two men. Only thing that wasn't as the man had said was that there weren't no space ship in the hole on the hill. They all figured that the alien-fish-people must have come and hid it before the sheriff got there. The sheriff and his men didn't know what to think. So, seein' as they couldn't prove the guy was guilty, they had to let him go. He went and lived back east until he died. And, the lake's been called Mystery Lake ever since."

Then Brent jumped back in. "And, if you're thinkin' that's a fairy-tale, think about this. Some years back, when my grandpa weren't yet old, he was a-fishin' out near the Rocky Reach area. He said it was good fishin' since it was raining a bit. But then, all's a sudden, it started pourin' and the wind blew up hard. His boat ended up sinkin' and he couldn't see for nothin' which way to swim. Soon, he just tuckered out. He said he went under ten times. Finally, he was ready to die.

"But then, he felt strong hands lift him up and pull him toward the shore. And he saw the dark faces of people beneath the waves. But, then, soon as he'd drug himself up on shore and turned to thank his rescuers, he found himself all alone. Nobody was there…nobody."

Joe laughed and said good-naturedly to Brent and Trent, "Well, whether it's true or not, you guys sure are good story tellers."

But Dru felt the hair on the back of his neck prickle up again as they turned to hurry back to the youth group. "Alien-fish-people…" he thought. "Did I really see one of the alien-fish-people?"

****

Enoch sat in anxious anticipation with the rest of the class of strappers. This was oral report week, and Elder Nathaniel was drawing lots to see who would give the first report. As their instructor held up a smooth green rock, James sighed out loud, and everyone else giggled with relief. Elder Nathaniel had pulled James' rock from the bag; therefore, today would be James' turn to give his oral report.

The instructor got up and smiled at James, motioning for him to take his place in the only chair in the room. All eyes turned eagerly to James, and James relaxed. He kind of enjoyed being the center of attention.

"Okay," James said, "I was assigned to look through the books in the library and talk with two Elders in order to prepare this oral report on the founding of Eden, our home.

"Let us see," James said, gathering his thoughts. "Way, way back in the 1800s, there was a man named Reverend Cameron Dickens. This American was a good man—not really an American, you know. He feared God, the Maker, and was what they called a *missionary*. Reverend Cameron also had a believing brother. His name was Connor Dickens.

"Together, Cameron and Connor had traveled far away from the cities and towns of their own people. They rode on large four-footed animals called *horses*. When they traveled, they had to climb giant mounds of dirt and rock, called *mountains*. And, they had to ride through seemingly endless patches of vegetation, called *forests*. Although they could see nothing but giant plants in front of them and behind them and all around them for days, they were not afraid. That is what they say it is like in some places up under the sun."

Enoch looked down at his hands as he felt his heart begin to beat fast. He had seen some of these giant plants with his own eyes when he had broken the forbidden barrier of the surface of the lake. Now, he felt the land of the sun calling to him again. Nearly every day, he had to remember Mrs. Bethany's words and not act in a rash manner. Every day, he looked up toward the lake surface and asked God, "Today? Can I go today?" But, since the day he had seen the American strapper, he had never again broken the 20-foot barrier. But, how he longed to. And now, listening to James, he longed to be hidden in the midst of a forest, traveling on the powerful, beautiful beast called a horse.

James continued, "Reverend Cameron and his brother settled close to a group of people they called *Indians*—people who had lived in the land long before the Americans had come. They had brown skin and straight black hair and dark eyes—like Mr. Gideon BearClaw, the father of Miriam. And, they lived right on the land above our Eden, where the hot springs flow up into the caves. They lived in a place that was covered with tall trees, where a thousand kinds of strange animals lived, including giant, dangerous cats called *cougars*.

"Well, together, the brothers worked with and taught the Indians. In time, many of the Indians became believing Christians. They even adopted Rev. Cameron and Mr. Connor as what they called their *blood brothers*. And, eventually, both Rev. Cameron and Mr. Connor took Indian maidens to be their wives.

"Well, as we know, there were thousands and thousands of sun-dwellers at that time. More than you could ever count. There were so many that hardly anybody knew anybody else anymore. And, many of the land-lovers stopped believing the words of the Holy Book. Instead, they did whatever they wanted to. So, many of the Americans began stealing land from the Indians. That made the Indians and Americans start to hate each other and hurt each other.

"Also, the Americans even started going to faraway places to steal people they called *Negroes* to do all their work for them. The Negroes were strong and tall, with dark skin, and tight curls in their hair, just like me," James added proudly.

Enoch looked around the group of strappers. They were all dark-skinned, though some not so dark as others. They were all dark, that is, except for him. Mimi seemed to sense what he was thinking and reached out to touch his hand.

"Anyway," James continued, "Reverend Cameron and Mr. Connor knew that taking the land of the Indians by force and making the Negroes into slaves was wrong. So, they began helping the Negroes escape to a land where it was against the law to have slaves. But, some of the Negroes just ended up staying in Eden with the Dickens and the Indians.

"Well, after a while, the Americans started to hate the Dickens brothers. They called them *traitors* and even tried to hurt them—even though the brothers were white-skinned and had yellow hair, like *they* did. Finally, around 1860, the Americans who wanted to keep Negroes as slaves started to fight and kill the Americans who did not think Negroes should be slaves. It became a very dangerous time for Reverend Cameron and their small town of Eden. It was dangerous because they lived with the Indians and had Negroes living right with them in their homes—as friends, not slaves.

"Then, after the Dickens' little town had been attacked twice, and many Indians harmed and even two Negroes stolen away, Reverend Cameron made a drastic decision. His Indian friends had shown him many hidden caverns that lay under our Emerald Lake. So, for a year, Reverend Cameron and his town worked and planned and prepared. They made many trips stocking the caverns below the lake in case they needed a place to hide for a time. Eventually, they had enough supplies to support the entire town for at least three months, maybe more.

"But one day, unexpectedly, a huge group of people came to Eden. They were all men, and they were all dressed exactly the same, and they all had weapons called *guns*. The people were called *soldiers*. These soldiers treated the Edenites as if they were their enemies—even though they had never harmed anyone. Well, everyone ran and tried to get to the lake, but most were taken away as prisoners. Even Mr. Connor Dickens was taken by the soldiers.

"However, Reverend Cameron and quite a few of the Edenites and their children did escape into Emerald Lake and made it down into the caverns. Six times, over the next two years, scouts went up and over to the neighboring areas to see what was happening in the land up above. But all they ever found was war and killing.

"So, even though Reverend Cameron and the Edenites had originally only planned to stay underground temporarily, they came to the decision to learn how to live permanently in the caverns. They decided to stay here forever—or at least until God, the Maker, told them it was safe to come back up to the land of the blazing sun."

With that, James stood up to give the instructor's seat back to Elder Nathaniel.

****

An eighth grader close to Billy was practically hopping off the ground in her excitement. "That is so neat! You mean those people *really* lived under the water?"

But, a boy had his eyebrows down and looked confused. "So, like, if the Edenites were really just people, where did the alien-fish-people go?"

Then Tasha Franklin jumped in. "But, how could've they lived in the caverns so long? What did they eat? How did…"

But, Billy just stood up with a laugh. "There's no time to give *all* the details. You'll just have to use your imaginations."

As the other kids started excitedly guessing how the story's plot would progress, David leaned over and whispered to Aaron, "D'you catch that? In Eden, the darker your skin, the *cooler* you are."

Aaron smiled and nodded. He was thinking that he kind of wished his family could've moved to Eden instead of Greenville.

Billy looked over at Aaron and winked. Then he glanced over at red-headed Todd who was looking thoughtfully at the ground.

"Okay," Billy said, "Mrs. Soure and Mrs. Avila are taking the *girls* up on the hill for the afternoon. You *boys* need to go with Mr. Soure and Mr. Avila. We'll all meet back at the mess tent for dinner at 5:30."

CHAPTER 5

After a time of discussion, Elder Nathaniel dismissed the strappers to go help their families with the daily chores. But, he called for Enoch to stay a moment.

"Yes, sir?" Eno asked a bit nervously. Elder Nathaniel was always kind, but at times, he could be stern.

Today, however, Elder Nathaniel just seemed to look at Enoch with a certain curiosity. Then, he put his hand on the strapper's shoulder and told him, "Boy, your father wants you at the fields right away. He has something important to talk about with you."

Out at the Lake Bottoms, Eno swam toward the Dickens family tulose fields. There, he found his father, Levi Dickens, planting the seedlings that would grow into the fall's harvest. Eno swam close to his dad and touched his shoulder in greeting. Mr. Levi smiled at his son and signed for him to follow him to a nearby bubble.

Inside the bubble, Eno and Mr. Levi sat on stones so that the upper part of their bodies were out of the water. Mr. Levi brought out some fish stew and peeka fruit to share with his son. They ate together in a comfortable silence, interrupted only briefly now and then by a passing Edenite needing to refill his or her lungs.

Mr. Levi cleared his throat and said in a bit of a serious tone, "Enoch, the Elders met together last night, and a herald was sent out to our home this morning."

Eno looked up in surprise at his dad. He felt a tide of fear and guilt rising swiftly in his gut. Had someone seen him swimming up by the lake surface? Would his father be chastised for his disobedience? "Why, Dad?" he asked a bit nervously. "What has happened? Is there anything wrong?"

Mr. Levi answered hesitantly, "Well, no. At least not yet. You see, my son, the old, peaceful American that has long owned the land above us is gone. The scouts have not seen him since the winter ice melted. And the scouts from the first of May saw both the blue and the brown dwellings lit up."

"So," Enoch responded, "I guess that means we will have to dim all the growing lights as they used to do when you were a small-fry, before the old man came, so that no Americans by the water will notice our lights."

Mr. Levi shook his head and said, "The Council has decided that we cannot afford to do that. Last winter, we almost ran out of food, even with the lights on bright. Each year, we need to grow more." Eno's dad continued, "They have talked this through for many days and have come to a conclusion." Mr. Levi stopped and looked thoughtfully at his son.

Eno dropped his eyes under his dad's look. "Uh, Dad," Eno said uncertainly, "there is something I need to tell you."

"No, Son," Mr. Levi said. "There is something I need to tell you, and to ask you."

"But, Dad," Eno looked into his father's face, "I feel I need to tell you this before you ask me anything."

Seeing Enoch's earnestness, Mr. Levi said, "Well, then, tell me what you have to say. I will listen."

"D-d-dad," Eno stammered, "I know you are going to be disappointed in me. I am sorry." Then he hurried on, "More than a month ago, I swam up to the surface of the lake and spent several minutes up by the blazing sun. I am sorry, really. I never planned to do it. It just sort of happened. But, it was like I had to do it. I long for the sun so much. I cannot explain it. But, you cannot imagine just how wonderful it is up there…"

"Enoch!" Mr. Levi nearly shouted. "Are you telling me that you have been past the forbidden zone and even broken through the surface of the lake?"

"Yes, sir." Enoch hung his head and waited for his father to assign him his deserved punishment.

However, Mr. Levi simply sat there and stared at his son until Eno finally looked up into his father's eyes. Eno expected to see anger and disappointment in his father's face. But instead, he saw a look of amazement and even satisfaction.

"Son," Mr. Levi said in a low voice, full of emotion, "you have indeed broken a very serious law among the Edenites. You might have put all of Eden in danger."

Enoch looked down again, feeling confused by his father's rebuking words. Not that the words were confusing—they were clear. He felt confused because his father's serious tone was underlined with something that sounded like…gladness.

"Enoch," his dad continued, "we will talk more of your disobedience later. For now, I will tell you what the herald from the Council told us this morning. The Council has decided that we must take the risk of finding out what kind of people the new Americans are. They have decided a non-threatening Edenite must go up and meet these new Americans."

"Wow!" Eno exclaimed. "I would do it in a minute. I am not afraid. I saw one of the American strappers. He looked just like me. I do not think he could be cruel or dangerous. But," Eno added with a sigh, "I am just a strapper. I know they will of course send one of the most experienced scouts, maybe Mr. Gideon."

"Eno," Mr. Levi said, "what you say is wise for what you know and understand. But the Council knows and understands much more. They have prayed many hours and have concluded that there is only one person that could meet the Americans without giving away his identity as an Edenite."

Eno looked a bit confused. He thought quickly through all the scouts, and Elders, and even some of the women, but couldn't think of anyone that seemed to be so special. He looked questioningly toward his dad. "Who is the one?" he asked.

His father's face filled with pride as he put his hands on Enoch's shoulders. "Son, it is you!"

Eno was shocked. "*Me!* The Council has chosen me? Why? Is it because I broke the rules and swam to the surface of the lake?"

"No, my boy," Mr. Levi said with a smile. "They said that it was the will of God that He made you with light skin and light hair and eyes. It is because your color, your features, and your size are those that are common to the Americans. The Council walks closely with God. They see that God made you different for a reason. It is their conclusion that God sent you, just as you are, at our time of need."

"Incredible…" was all Eno could think of to say.

Mr. Levi continued, "At first, I was uncertain. Your mother and I prayed, but we could not feel sure that we should allow you to be exposed to such danger. If only we could be sure of the will of God…" Then, Eno's dad laughed and said, "Now, my boy, I *am* sure! And I can send you, trusting in the good plan of the Maker."

"But, how, Dad?" Eno asked. "How can you be so sure?"

"You, yourself, settled it for me, Eno," his dad said with another laugh. "When you told me that you long for the sun, and that you thought what is above the water is the most wonderful place…the Creator was telling me: 'Yes, Enoch is the one I have chosen in our time of need.'"

Enoch's feelings were swirling up and down and every which way. He hardly knew what to say. Finally, his father said in a calmer voice, "Of course, my son, the decision is yours. You do not have to go. What does the Maker speak to your heart?"

Eno grabbed his dad's hand and said, "Mrs. Bethany said that I must wait for God to speak to me, that I must follow His plan. Now, I *know* His plan. I feel like I am finally set free—free to do what everything inside of me has been longing to do! Yes, Father, I want to do it."

"Well, then," Mr. Levi said, "we should go at once and talk with the Council. They are expecting us."

****

Ana walked slowly up the dusty path, going nowhere in particular. It was a hot July afternoon. She tried to tell herself she didn't care if Christy had already been to three different birthday parties that summer, while she hadn't even been invited to one.

Anyway, the problem didn't seem to be the kids now. They had all been treating her pretty normal now. It seemed like it was the parents that weren't so sure they could trust her. Ana just didn't get it. She hadn't been born more than an eight hour drive from where the Hill Valley kids had been born. But the grown-ups around Hill Valley acted like having dark skin meant you were born weird or bad or something.

Coming around a bend in the path, Ana headed out into the fields, out toward Mystery Lake. Her thoughts went back to the story her brother, Josiás, had told her about the alien-fish-people. "What a joke," she thought to herself. "I'm no superstitious country bumpkin! I'm not afraid to go out to Rocky Reach."

Actually, since their first week in Hill Valley, neither the Sanders nor the Garcia kids had been back to Rocky Reach. It was just a bit too far away. Besides, Dru never seemed to want to go out that way again anyway. So, they had just been swimming off the pier closer to home. But, for some reason, Ana felt like she was proving something by going all the way back to Rocky Reach…alone.

Once Ana came to the rocky outcrop by the lake, she walked deliberately up the path that led to the high ledge her cousin Dru had jumped off of almost two months before. Once on the ledge, Ana sat down and carefully peeked over the edge. "Good grief," she thought. "How had Dru ever gotten the nerve to make that jump?"

Then, unexpectedly, Ana caught sight of something moving below her in the water. It looked like Dru. And, he wasn't coming up! He just stayed there under the surface! "Dear God," Ana prayed, "Dru's under the water. Is he dead? What should I do?" Suddenly, she knew what she must do. Flinging off her shoes, Ana made herself jump off the ledge—down…down…down where she might just have time to save her cousin from drowning.

As soon as she hit the water, Ana spread out her arms and legs to keep herself from going too deep. And, as quickly as she could, she swam up toward the boy floating near the surface.

But, by the time she reached him, she saw that he was now upright with his head out above the water. "That Dru!" she thought. "He did that on purpose, just to scare me!" Angry as a hornet, Ana pushed herself up partially out of the water and grabbed hold of the boy's arm and swung him around to face her.

"How dare you play such a mean trick on me, Andru San…" Ana started to say, but never finished. Instead, she flung herself away from the boy in extreme embarrassment.

It *wasn't* Dru. It was some other boy she had never met before. "Oh, no!" she thought. "What an idiot he must think I am."

Out loud, she said, "Hey, man, I'm really sorry. I mean, I thought you were my cousin. And, you know, I thought you were hurt or something. Then, like, I thought you were my cousin playing a mean joke on me or something. Really, I'm sorry."

The boy's face was a picture of complete surprise and curiosity. He drew his eyebrows together and said in amazement, "Why, Miss, you have dark skin."

Ana's temper came back a bit and she frowned at the boy. "Well, duh!" she said. "And you have white skin. So what's the big deal?"

"Well…" the boy said in some confusion, "Umm, I guess I thought all the, uh, people who lived here, uh, had light skin."

"Whatever!" Ana said. But it was hard to stay mad at someone who seemed so entirely genuine. So, she added, "Anyway, most people in Hill Valley are white. My family's new here." Then, with a half-smile, she said, "My name's Ana Garcia. And, I don't know about you, but I'm getting exhausted treading water out here. Let's get back to shore."

Enoch hadn't even thought about getting tired. To him, treading water was as natural as walking was to Ana. But, he swam to the shore and pulled himself up and out of the water. Eno had been to the lake surface every day for a week. However, he had only pulled himself out of the water twice. He felt excited, but also vulnerable. His body was so heavy and limited out of the water. Looking up, he felt he would never get over the fact that there was no water or cavern ceiling above him.

Ana watched him curiously. He looked like a lot of the Hill Valley boys, though he lacked the usual tan. But, something was really different about him. He acted like he was from another planet or something. "Say," she asked in a friendly tone, "where'd you get those wild swimming clothes? I've never seen anything like 'em."

Enoch looked down at his thelpa-fiber shirt and shorts. They were just simple and modest. They were made more to be practical than for their looks. His shirt was dyed in a striped pattern of a dirty green and off-white. The colors and pattern together indicated at a glance that he belonged to the Dickens family line. His shorts were dyed a burnt red, indicating which of the three cities of Eden he was from.

Eno answered her question simply and truthfully. "My mother made them for me." Then, he asked Ana, "Your clothes are so bright and clean. Did your mother make them for you?"

"No, way!" Ana said shaking her head with a laugh. "So, what's your name, anyway?"

"I am Enoch, the son of Levi of the family of Dickens, and Rachel of the family of Baker," Eno answered in the formal Edenite way of introducing oneself.

Ana shook her head again. She was thinking, "This guy is totally bizarre." But, she didn't want to hurt his feelings, so she just asked, "So, Enoch, where do you come from? I've never heard an accent like yours before—and, back in Huron, I knew people from all over the world."

"Well," Enoch said hesitatingly, "I guess I come from… around here. Everyone in my family speaks the way I do. Does everyone by the lake speak the way you do?" he asked.

"Pretty much," Ana said. "Though I guess my family and my uncle's family speak more like city folks than the Hill Valley country folks do." Then she asked, "So, is your family gonna stay around here for the summer?"

"Yes," Eno answered with a smile. Then he added, "Maybe we can get to know one another and be friends."

Ana was about to say, "That could be fun," when she saw a sudden look of fear cross Eno's face. Turning around to see what he was seeing, Ana saw the Sanders' family dog, a big ol' yellow lab, galloping happily toward them. "Don't worry, he's nice…" Ana started to say as she turned back to her new friend. But Enoch was gone.

Ana looked all around her, then stood up to look around a few rocks, but she couldn't see where Enoch might have gone. By then, the dog had reached Ana and was sniffing all around where Eno had been seated. Then, he stood at the edge of the lake and barked at the water. He looked up at Ana, then back at the water and barked again.

"Well, Loopner, ol' boy, I guess you're right," Ana said to the dog. "He must have just slid back into the water and swam away." Looking around once more, and then back at the water, she said with a laugh, "Maybe there are alien-fish-people after all." Then the hairs on her arms tingled, and she wasn't sure if she was joking or not. "Boy! He was, ah… different. That's for sure." She looked back over at the water one more time. Then she patted the dog and said, "Come on, let's get on home."

****

Tasha Franklin looked thoughtful. "So, Ana got to meet someone that seemed even more *different* than she was…I mean, when she met Enoch, she thought he was, like, *from a different planet*—just like the white folks from the country town treated her because she was black."

Abel spoke up in the nasal tones of Steve Urkel, the super-nerdy brain from a popular TV sitcom. "Different usually isn't bad. Sometimes, it's even good."

Everyone in the circle turned their eyes on Abel and Darin. They certainly weren't your average teenage boys.

"Yeah, but, you don't want to be *too* different," Todd pointed out, "or people think you're just weird or strange or something."

Tasha got mad. "Hey! Just like I can't help being black, Abel can't help having Asperger Syndrome. I think it's *dumb* that everybody feels like they have to dress and act the same."

Todd held up his hands in self-defense. "Wait, I didn't mean that the way it sounded. I just meant…well, I guess I just meant…hmmm, I guess I don't know what I really meant."

As Tasha started to make another angry response, Abel put his hand on her arm and said in an earnest tone, "It's my really and true real opinion that God made people as social beings. I totally think that He really made us to want to get along with each other. I guess this could be why most people want to *fit in* with the rest of the crowd. So, Todd, what you said is really a *natural* expression of how most people feel."

Then Darin spoke up. "People that most everybody calls 'normal' seem to have a built-in ability to read how other people are feeling. This ability enables most folks to behave in a way that makes everyone feel comfortable—at least, if they want to."

Abel stood up and pulled his pants high up on his stomach and turned his feet out. Then he put on his best Steve Urkel smile. "It's all in the body language…"

Even Tasha relaxed and smiled at Abel's great Urkel imitation.

"The problem is," Billy said more seriously, "that many people with autistic traits, such as Asperger Syndrome, don't seem to have this ability to read how people are feeling. So, they can't easily learn how to *fit in,* and they are confused and hurt that people won't be friends with them."

Darin quickly jumped up opposite of Abel's *Steve* character and struck an ultra-cool pose, holding a non-existent cigarette between his finger and thumb. "Hey, Steve-man, you are such a nerd."

"Yep!" Steve smiled. "Do you want to be my friend?"

"No way, ya geek!" Mr. Cool responded.

Then, Darin *morphed* into a reserved, wealthy man brushing off his non-existent tailored suit and straightening his $200 imported silk tie. "Mr. Urkel, can't you see that your behavior makes people uncomfortable?"

Steve's smile faded, and he pushed up his imaginary goggle glasses. "Well, I like everyone. And I thought everyone liked me." Then, he walked over to Mr. Snob and got right up close in his face. "I like you. Do you want to be my friend?"

Mr. Snob quickly backed up several steps and said in an embarrassed tone, "I'm sorry, I'm afraid I'm too, uh…too busy."

Abel put on a sad and lonely expression, and said in Steve's nasally voice, "I don't understand why people don't want to be my friend."

All the kids by Billy's pond looked down at the ground. Everyone felt a little uncomfortable. Each of them had shied away from someone 'different' at one time or another. Then, Dinah Soure, who had just joined them, walked straight over to 'Steve' and put her arm across his shoulders. "I'll be your friend," she said enthusiastically.

'Steve' smiled his trademark smile and was so happy that he snorted through his nose. Then, he put his arm through hers and started to drag her along with him, saying, "I'm so glad. We'll be the best of friends…Now, let me tell you all about my latest experiment on cosmic inter-planetary gravitational-replicating photon acceleration."

Everyone laughed. But, as everyone stood up and stretched, Billy carried the conversation one step deeper. "You see, everyone is different, but everyone has the *need* to feel a part of some group. We need this because we were created as social beings. This emotional/psychological need to be accepted by others is a like a mirror image of our spiritual need to be accepted by God. We were created as social beings first and foremost because God wanted to have a relationship with us—He wants to be our Father and our Friend."

"Wow," Todd and Aaron both said at the same time. Then they looked at each other and smiled. It was a good moment. It was a moment that made it clear that red-headed, white Todd, and tall, black Aaron were both feeling exactly the same on the *inside*.

Then, Mrs. Soure called back to the others, "Come on y'all, the dino-dig is all set up and waiting."

CHAPTER 6

Joe leaned toward his pony's neck and urged him to go faster. With a grin, he yelled back to Ana, "Paco can beat your Rosa any day!" Joe's new pony was nearly twelve, but still enjoyed a frisky ride. Joe felt like laughing out loud as the hot August air rushed past him. Moving from Huron to Hill Valley hadn't been too easy for Joe. Everything was just so different. But Paco made it all worth it.

"Hey, Josiás!" Ana yelled. "Slow down!" Ana's pony was only eight, but she acted 18, which suited Ana just fine. Ana loved riding just as much as Joe—she just wasn't into the crazy stuff.

Joe turned his white and brown speckled pony in a wide circle and pulled him up next to his sister's golden mare. "Come on, Ana, the quicker we get out to Rocky Reach, the more time we'll have with Eno. You know how excited he is about seeing the ponies."

"He *is* really excited," Ana agreed with a smile. "But, no matter how slow we go on horses, it's faster than walking. So, let's just trot along. Mom said we don't have to be back until 8:00."

Once they were close to Mystery Lake, they both slid off their ponies and tied them by a shady cluster of trees. Then they raced to the water's edge and jumped right in. They swam past a sandy-colored boulder, then toward a sharp rock that cut out into the water. Then, they climbed back out of the water and ran past the next six large stones to a small shelter made from the cliffs and ledges. "Eno! Are you here? Eno?"

Out from the shade of the ledges, Enoch instantly appeared. "Ana! Joe! I am so pleased you could come!" Then he continued a bit more seriously, "I am afraid I can only stay for one hour today. My uncle's children are sick and they need my help in the fields."

"Wow, man," Joe said, "I didn't know your uncle lived around here. What's his name?"

Enoch looked a bit uncomfortable and answered, "I doubt you would know him." Then, he hurriedly added, "Were you able to bring your horses?"

Ana smiled and said, "Of course. Come on!" All three then ran a bit down the shore and jumped back into the water where they swam past the jutting rock and the sandy-colored boulder. Then, where the rocks stopped dominating the shore, they hopped out.

In the water, Enoch always far out-swam Ana and Joe. However, on land, Ana and Joe easily reached the ponies ahead of Eno. "Wow, man," Eno said, trying to talk like Joe. "They are so big. Are you not afraid of them?"

Joe started to laugh, but Ana shushed him. "Well, Eno," she said, "some horses are kind of rough and dangerous. But our little horses are just sweet and gentle. They wouldn't hurt anyone, unless they were very frightened."

Ana and Joe were both stroking their pony's noses. So Eno worked up his nerve to walk closer. Reaching out his hand, he touched Rosa's neck. "Amazing," he said. "I can feel its strength just by touching it."

"Do you want to try to ride?" Joe asked.

"Oh, yes!" Enoch answered excitedly. "However," he added, "please stay right beside me, Joe."

Ana hopped up into Rosa's saddle to show Eno how to get into Paco's. Then she showed him what to do with his feet and with the reins. And Joe took hold of Paco's bridle and led him forward.

"Ana?" Eno questioned seriously. "Do I look more like a cowboy or an Indian or a missionary now that I am riding a horse?" In Eden's library he had read that cowboys, Indians, and missionaries all traveled on horseback.

Ana and Joe were getting used to Eno's strange questions, so she just laughed and said, "None of the above right now! You look more like a sack of potatoes in that saddle."

Joe jumped in. "Know what, Eno? Papa called home last night. He and Uncle Christopher plan to be home by the end of the week. And Dru said they're pretty sure they'll find the horses they want at the show this weekend. They plan to buy another horse for our family and three for Dru's family. If they can find some good deals, we'll have an extra horse for you to learn to ride by yourself. Wouldn't that be fun?"

Enoch could hardly believe it. He looked toward the lake and said, "I wish Miriam could come and ride a horse, too."

"Who's Miriam?" Ana asked.

Again, Eno looked a little awkward. "Well, she is my best friend," he said hesitantly. Then he added, "I guess she was my only real friend until I met you two." And, he went on in a hurry, "Can I ask you guys something? Why are you so nice to me? I am as white as the belly of a trout, but you treat me as if I were nice and dark just like you are."

Joe and Ana looked at Eno's earnest face and shrugged their shoulders. "Why shouldn't we be nice to you?" Ana asked. "It doesn't matter what color you are. People are just people."

Then Joe said, "You act as if you wish you were dark like us."

"Does not everyone?" Eno asked innocently.

"Not Brent and Trent, anyway," Joe said, remembering his last meeting with the two cousins a few days before. The words *Chico* and *Shorty* still rang in his ears. "Well, I guess I wouldn't want to be anything I'm not. But, it sure would be easier if I were white like you and as tall and strong as you and Dru are."

As Joe turned Paco to the side, Enoch almost fell out of his saddle in surprise. "What! Do you mean you…you Americans would rather be white?"

"No!" Ana answered a bit defensively. "I don't want to be white. I want to be just what I am. Anyway, there are a lot more non-white people in the world than there are white people—a whole lot more." Then she continued, "It doesn't really make any sense, but—at least here in America—I guess white folks have just been in the majority for a long time." Then, she asked curiously, "What country does your family come from, anyway?"

"I will tell you soon," Eno promised, then asked, "Do I look like your cousin, Dru?"

"Kinda," Joe answered. "You're both tall and white, with blond hair and all."

"You think I am tall?" Eno asked in some amazement.

"Well, at least compared to us," Ana answered with a smile.

Enoch thought for a minute while Joe led Paco back to the grove of trees. "Can I meet your cousins sometime?" he asked.

"Sure," Ana answered. "They'll be home the day after tomorrow. When does your family leave Hill Valley?"

"Oh, I do not think very soon," Eno said. Then he carefully climbed down out of Paco's saddle. He looked into

Paco's big eyes and stroked his long nose. "I will come here on Friday at 9:00 in the morning. Please bring your cousins if you can." Then, as he reached the water's edge, he told them, "I must go home now. My uncle needs me. Do not worry that I swim so long in the water. I will be fine." And he jumped into the lake and swam away toward a large curve that led out into a wider section of Mystery Lake.

"Man!" Joe said, "I bet nobody in the world can swim as well as Eno can!" Again, how surprised Enoch would have been if he had heard Joe's exclamation.

****

"So, cowboy, you think this is the horse for you?" A tall city-looking man in some bought-for-the-occasion country duds was talking to Mr. Tomás Garcia. "He's a good one—old enough to have calmed down, young enough to have years of ride left in him."

Dru watched his Uncle Tito handle the bay horse with obvious pleasure. Mr. Green, the horse's owner, had run a prosperous riding ranch just outside the city. But, as the city had spread out, the developers had offered Mr. Green a price for his land that he just couldn't refuse. So, he had come to the fair with several horses he was eager to get off his hands.

Mr. Garcia slid down off the horse and patted its neck. "Yes, sir, Mr. Green. Flicker, here, has just the right feel for my family." Then, he reached into his pocket and pulled out his wallet. Looking at Mr. Green, Uncle Tito asked, "Will a check be okay?"

Mr. Green looked a bit uncomfortable and said, "Sorry, mister, but I can only accept cash or a money order."

Uncle Tito looked into Mr. Green's face, but Mr. Green wouldn't meet his eyes. "I'm afraid I don't have that much cash," Uncle Tito said. "How about a credit card?"

"Well, now," Mr. Green cleared his throat nervously, "I'd like to sell you this here mare, but I'm afraid I can only accept cash or a money order."

Dru saw the color rise in his uncle's face. But he simply slipped his wallet back into his pocket and said, "Well, Mr. Green, Flicker's a good horse. I'll see what I can do." And he turned and walked over to Dru.

Dru and Uncle Tito walked for a bit without talking. Finally, Dru asked in a confused tone, "Uh, Uncle Tito, Dad just bought Beauty from Mr. Green with a check. Why won't he let you buy Flicker with a check?"

Uncle Tito tried to smile. "Well, Dru, Mr. Green is a rich older guy from town. I'm guessing he hasn't had much contact with Latino folks. And, there's a good chance that he's just heard negative news about the growing Hispanic gangs and all. I guess he doesn't feel he can trust me."

"But," Dru said in disbelief, "that's like totally prejudiced! I sure wouldn't buy his horse if I were you! And, I'm gonna tell Dad he shouldn't buy Beauty either!"

Mr. Garcia put his arm across Dru's shoulder. "Yes, I guess it is prejudice. But, you can't completely blame Mr. Green. Think about it," he went on. "What are the images of Latino people Mr. Green sees on TV? Poor, uneducated, violent. He just hasn't had a chance to have some positive relationships with regular, honest Latinos. So, it's hard for him to trust me."

"Then," Dru said, "shouldn't you go tell him that you're as good as he is—that it doesn't matter if you're black or brown or white, as long as you're honest? I mean, he's gotta learn sometime."

Uncle Tito shook his head. "In rare situations, you might be able to do that. However, usually the best thing to do is just to *show* these people that you are just as good as they are. In this case, I remain polite and calm. I could choose not to buy from him. But, I think it is better to show him that I am an honest man with the funds to pay for his horse. That way, I will be leaving only a positive image of Latinos in his mind."

"I think you should just go to the seller next to Mr. Green and buy Tonto—and pay for him with cash!" Dru said with a vindictive tone. "That way, Mr. Green will see that he lost out just because he was prejudiced."

Uncle Tito laughed and slapped Dru on the shoulder. "Well, Dru, honestly, I already thought of that. It would give me a certain satisfaction to see his disappointment. But," he went on, "in the end, that would only leave him with a frustrated, negative feeling toward me—and maybe toward other Latinos. So, I think it's better for me to just go get a money order. Besides, Flicker's a better horse than Tonto. I shouldn't let bad feelings guide me into making an unwise purchase, should I? If I did, then, no matter what, I would lose."

"Yeah, I guess you're right," Dru agreed. Then he caught sight of his dad coming toward them and shouted out, "Hey, Dad! Uncle Tito found the best horse ever. And, it was one of Mr. Green's, so it's one of Beauty's old friends. Isn't that great?"

****

After the others had headed out, Todd stayed behind. Kicking a rock nervously, he asked, "Uh, Mr. James…Billy, can I ask a question?"

"Of course, Todd," Billy answered. "That's why we're here."

"Well, you know…well, my dad's sister, uh, married a black man from the East Side. Anyway, I guess he's okay and all. I mean, my aunt likes him…" Todd stopped and tried to figure out just what to say. Then he continued, "Anyway, neither my dad nor my grandpa have spoken to my aunt since she married, uh, her husband. They say that God made whites to marry whites and blacks to marry blacks. They say that blacks are people and all, just not the same as whites. They say that interracial marriages just cause trouble. Grandpa even said that it says right in the Bible that people shouldn't intermarry."

Billy sighed. Just the little bit Todd had said was full of so much hurt. It was sad. "Todd, when God talked about intermarriage, He was speaking specifically to the Israelites. He was concerned with building a specific priestly nation. He was protecting the Israelites from being influenced by the evil practices of the nations around them. He wasn't saying one kind of person was better than another."

Todd looked out over the ErinWood pond, then went on. "Dad says that whites marrying blacks is like a cat marrying a dog. It just ain't right."

Billy's mouth grew serious. He himself took a moment to look out at the pond, trying to keep control of his temper. Finally, he looked at Todd. "Man, that makes no sense! Your mom has black hair. Your dad is blond. They got married and had you—a red-head. Does different color make a different species?" Billy shook his head. "That's outright ridiculous! Think about it. A cat is a cat. A black cat is a cat. A small black cat with short hair is just as much a cat as a big white cat with long hair. No one would ever say different."

With another sigh, Billy put his arm around Todd's shoulder. "Todd, I know it's hard. You love your dad. You should. And, your dad is a good, honest, hard-working man. It's just that he's talking what his dad taught him to say. And, your grandpa is talking what his dad taught him to say.

"But now, it's your turn. Are you gonna just keep on talking what prejudice has taught them to say? Or are you gonna look for the truth? People are people are people. Tall or short, black or white, fat or thin, fast or slow, young or old, athletic or handicapped…they are all people…all made in God's image."

Todd still wasn't sure how to feel. "I know you're right." He shook his head. "Still, there are so many cultural differences and all that…"

"You're right," Billy said. "Cultural differences can cause some real misunderstandings. It's something that has to be carefully considered. Still, two white folks can come from entirely different cultures, too. Even they will have to adjust to each other. It's important to realize that some different ethnic groups have been separated for thousands of years. So, now that cultures are mixin', it's gonna take a while for people to get past tradition and color, and just see people as people—equal before God and equal before each other."

Todd nodded. "Thanks, Billy, that helped." Then, he ran off to find the others.

CHAPTER 7

Dru was unusually quiet as he walked with his cousins toward Rocky Reach. Ana and Joe had told him all about the fun they had had in the last couple of weeks with their curious new friend—Enoch.

Over and over in the past months, Dru had remembered the strange pale face of the boy he had seen deep down in Mystery Lake. During the summer, his cousins had often suggested going back out to Rocky Reach, where he had seen the fish boy. But Dru had always made up some kind of excuse. And, since he was the oldest, no one had argued with him. Now, they were all on their way to Rocky Reach to meet a boy who seemed to have appeared out of nowhere, who could swim like a fish, and, as Ana said, seemed like he was from another planet or something.

"Come on, Dru," Joe called back. "Eno's probably already there waiting."

Dru reached down to give Loopner a pat. He had purposely brought his big lab along just in case...well, just in case. Straightening up, he called to Joe, "Betcha I win!" and took off running.

At the lake, Loopner was the first one in the water. He seemed to know right where they were heading. One by one the three cousins jumped in after him—by the big boulder, around the projecting rock, then up on the beach and past the big rocks. Before they got there, Dru heard Loopner's excited whines and a boy giggling. "Oh, Loopner, stop! You are so much bigger than my little Leah! You almost knocked me down."

Dru got to the little rocky hideaway first and found Loopner enthusiastically greeting a boy about his own age. When the boy looked up and saw Dru, his smile faded. Both boys stood still. They knew that they had seen each other before.

Dru took a step backwards, but bumped into Ana who had stepped up behind him. "Hey, Dru," she said, "this is Enoch."

Dru felt like turning and running. All his fears and late night thoughts of alien-fish-people flashed into his mind, sending his adrenaline into high gear.

Joe was staring at Dru. "Hey, man, what's wrong. You look like you saw a ghost or something."

At this, Enoch stepped forward. "Uh, Joe, I think I can explain. A couple of months ago, Dru and I already met. Well, actually, just saw each other, really. We were in the lake, down under the water. Maybe he thought I drowned or something, since he did not know how well I can swim."

Suddenly, Dru felt very foolish. How stupid could he be? Duh! He had spent so much time thinking about Brent and Trent's alien-fish-people story, and so much time imagining all sorts of weird things, that he had brainwashed himself into believing something totally ridiculous.

Pretty embarrassed, Dru tried to smile. "Hey, man, sorry I acted so crazy. Joe and Ana have told me about all the cool things you've been showing them." Then, turning toward the lake, he said, "Let's go have some fun!"

For the next two hours, the four kids played together in the water. Getting his courage up, Dru even showed Eno how to jump off the high ledge. And Ana, having already jumped off once, was ready to do it again. Even Joe finally did it. Funny how fear can turn into fun. Over and over, they each took turns jumping, quite unaware that they were being watched from behind a small group of trees.

Finally, Eno pulled himself up on shore and told his friends, "I am afraid I must be going. I am still needed in the fields. These days, it seems, many people are sick."

Dru and Ana looked at each other and seemed to read each other's thoughts. "Hey, Eno," Ana said, "our parents told us we could stay out for quite a while. We'd be happy to come and help you in your uncle's fields."

Enoch looked down into the lake for a long while. Finally, he answered, "You are very kind. I will tell the Counc…I mean, my family what you have said. But, I do not think you will be allowed to come…but, maybe someday." With that, Eno slid into the water and began to swim out toward the deeper, wider section of the lake.

Dru watched him swim away with many questions in his mind. Enoch was certainly different than anyone he had ever met. But, one thing he knew for sure, he wasn't an alien-fish-person—he was just a kid.

****

Christiana Sanders was ten, but looked more like seven. When she had been three, she had caught a serious case of *Shotsie*. The doctors said that she had used all her strength to get well and hadn't had any strength left to grow with. But, although she was small, Christy refused to be grouped with the *little cousins*. They were hardly more than babies. So, she had learned to keep up with the *big kids* without complaining. And, although she was not exceptionally brave, she was determined to do whatever they did. That was why she now stood high on the rocky ledge above the emerald waters after all the others had headed home.

Christy had been all ready to hike out to Rocky Reach with her brother and cousins to meet their new friend. But, for some reason, Dru had seemed totally against her going. He almost always welcomed her along, unless he thought it might be too dangerous for her. Sometimes, he was a bit over-protective. Dru hadn't had any good reason to say she couldn't come, so he had just bribed her. He had promised her she could have first pick of the ponies the next day if she stayed home and weeded the back garden for him. She had reluctantly agreed. Then, she had run straight out to the garden and worked like a whip to finish it all in a hurry. After that, she had walked herself out to Rocky Reach.

Christy had made it to the slim section of the lake about 15 minutes before Enoch had swam off. But, instead of just swimming over to her bigger cousins, Christy had decided to hide and watch for a while. She felt pretty sure that Dru would be angry about her coming, especially alone. While she had watched, she saw them all jumping off the ledge, squealing with glee.

Now, walking toward the edge, she thought about her parents' rule: *No swimming alone*. "Anyway," she said to herself, "I won't be swimming. Not really. I'll just jump in and then do a little swim to get out." Her conscience called her a cheater. But, she had made up her mind to break the rule. So…she jumped.

As soon as she began to fall, Christy knew she had made a big mistake. At first, she was frozen with fear. Then, even before she hit the water, she began to panic. She flapped her arms and kicked her legs. Her body began to tip, and she flipped sideways. Then, *whap!* She hit the water hard. Christy felt the air being crushed out of her. And there was no time to take a new breath before she went under. Down she went. In her mind, she knew she should be kicking and swimming up. But her entire body seemed stunned. She just kept sinking down. Her need for air was painful now, but she couldn't move. Her head began to spin, then she closed her eyes.

At that moment, she felt a hand take hold of her. She was so relieved. "It must be Dru," she thought. It was odd that she felt like he was pulling her downward, rather than upward. But, she trusted him and tried to hold her breath a few more seconds.

Then, other hands were grabbing and pulling. Finally, her head was breaking out of the water. She gasped for air. She had no strength to hold herself up. But, the others held her above the water until she had taken in all the air she needed. Soon, she began to take notice of what was around her. There was no bright sunlight, no rocky ledges, and no grassy fields. Instead, she was in a moderately lit cavern. It smelled strongly of fish. And, there seemed to be small birds fluttering and chirping overhead.

Twisting around she questioned, "Dru, where are we?" But she immediately saw that it was not Dru who was holding her. On her right, she saw a long dark face. It was the face of a boy. But he was more like a man in size. And he was breathing heavily, as if nearly worn out. Turning to her left, she saw a dark-faced girl. Her hair was curly and black, and pulled tightly back from her face. The girl was breathing easily, as if she saved people from drowning all the time.

Christy was not afraid—these two kids had just rescued her. Besides, she had never heard the stories about alien-fish-people. So, she smiled and said, "Wow! Thanks so much for helping me. I think you saved my life!" Then, she added, "My name is Christiana Sanders. Who are you?"

The boy pushed away from Christy and said to the girl, "Do not tell her anything. Do not say a word!" He shivered and tried to catch his breath. Then, in an angry tone, he added, "I cannot believe you did this, Miriam! If trouble comes to us, it will be your fault, not mine!"

While Miriam helped a confused Christy swim over to the relatively dry cavern floor, she tried to calm the boy down. "Come now, James, you know we could not let her die. We had to save her. The Elders have said that it is the right thing to do."

"Be quiet, I said," James said sharply. "She is nothing but an American. She can be nothing but bad news. Now, do not say anything to her—nothing—until I go and get someone who knows what to do." With that, the boy ducked under the water and swam away.

Christy looked at Miriam and said, "I'm sorry I made your brother mad. I really shouldn't have jumped from so high. Still, I'm so glad you helped me."

Miriam answered with a laugh. "Goodness, Miss Christiana, James is not my brother. And I do not care if he is mad or not. Besides, he did not have to help. So, I guess under all of his hot air, he is really glad that you are okay."

Christy felt a little uneasy. "Why wouldn't he want me to be okay?" And, looking around, she added, "Where are we, anyway?"

"Do not worry, my friend," Miriam encouraged her. "But, I suppose I should not talk too much until the adults come with their better understanding of what we should do." Then, looking at Christy's white-blond hair, she said, "My, how bleached your hair is. Even Enoch's hair is not so light."

Christy looked at Miriam in surprise. "Do you know Enoch? My brother and cousins are friends with him. I haven't met him, but I saw him today."

Miriam reached out to touch Christy's hair. "Yes," she said, "Enoch is my best friend. I was waiting for him to return when you fell into the lake." Then she added, "Enoch has told me that some of you Americans have skin as dark as mine. Is that true?"

"Americans?" Christy asked in a puzzled tone. "Aren't you an American?"

Miriam hesitated, uncertain if she should answer Christy's question. "Well, we live not far from you and your friends. But, we have never considered ourselves Americans. I mean, Americans are a warring people, and our people desire peace."

Christy wasn't sure what to say to that. Miriam seemed nice and all, but she didn't really make much sense. So, she said, "I don't really know what you mean. But, I don't think anyone likes war—no matter what color they are."

Suddenly, almost silently, four heads appeared near the two girls. One was a man. One was a woman. Then there was James. And the last one was Enoch.

****

A boy close to Billy spoke up, "Man, I think it's weird that the Edenites think Americans are, well, bad guys and all." Then he laughed and said, "Aren't Americans supposed to be the good guys?"

A girl added, "Yeah, it feels uncomfortable to hear James and those guys talk about Americans like we're some kind of cruel, mean people."

Billy nodded. "Good. That's what I want it to feel like. You see, all the *Edenites* really know about the *Americans* is that they made blacks into slaves, stole land from the Native Americans, and fought against, and killed, their own people." Billy sighed. "All that—unfortunately—*is* part of America's history. It's just that the Edenites didn't know much about some of the good we've done. So, the bad is what molded their view of Americans. You can't really blame them, can you—even if this view is outdated and not completely accurate?"

Todd cleared his throat a bit nervously. "Um…you know, sometimes we hear things about people that make us think badly about them. Some of it might be true. But, a lot of it isn't true anymore or maybe wasn't ever true. But, still, it kinda messes up all your thinking. It's hard to see past the stuff you *think* is true, and just see the for-real facts." Todd stopped and smiled shyly at Aaron, then continued, "But I think it's really important not to just hold onto what we've heard, but to really take the time to find out what is actually true."

"Right on!" Billy agreed. "If we're willing to do that, then we'll be able to see past our differences and see what we have in common—first and foremost, that we are all people, created in God's image."

CHAPTER 8

"Come on, boy!" Dru called to Loopner. "No time to chase rabbits." As the three cousins were walking home from their visit with Enoch, Loopner kept trying to go back. He would sniff the ground and whine. Then, he would look at Dru as if to say, "Hey, we need to go back this way."

"I guess he didn't get all his swimming out," Joe said with a laugh. "He is a Labrador, you know."

Ana called to him, "It's okay, Loop! We'll go again in a few days." But, the dog just looked at them and whined. Finally, he barked and took off back toward Rocky Reach.

Dru wasn't sure what to think. The three of them just stood there for a minute. Then Dru said, "Well, he knows his way home. I guess he'll come when he's ready." With that, they all turned toward home.

After saying goodbye to Ana and Joe, Dru turned into the lane that led to the Sanders' house. Once inside, he found his mom at work in the kitchen. "Hey, Mom," he said, grabbing one of the grapes she was washing for lunch. "Where's Christy? I thought she'd be out in the garden."

Mrs. Sanders stopped her work and looked at Dru. "Honey, Christy did the weeding and then ran to join you guys." Then she asked with a note of concern, "Didn't you at least meet her on your way home?"

Dru shook his head. "No, Mom. Really, we never saw her. And we stayed right on the path."

Mrs. Sanders rubbed her temples the way she always did when she was worried, then said to Dru, "I'm gonna need you to go and find her. Go ahead and take one of the ponies, you're probably pretty tired after that long walk and swimming and all."

"Sure, Mom," Dru said. He thought it was pretty cool that he was gonna get to ride Azúl, even before getting all his chores done.

When Dru was almost to the cluster of trees by Rocky Reach, he heard Loopner barking. It was a frantic kind of a bark. Dru urged Azúl forward and rode right up to the water's edge. Over along the shore, Dru saw Loopner up on the high rocky ledge he and his friends had been jumping off of earlier that day. "Come on, Loopner," he called. "That's too high for you to jump from. Come on, I need you to help me find Christy."

Loopner cocked his head at Dru, then started barking again. "Loopner! Come on, boy! Let's go find Christy." At this, Loopner reached down and picked something up in his mouth, then started down the rocky path off the ledge.

Dru started to get a strange feeling running up and down his spine. He hopped off Azúl and ran to meet Loopner, not really sure why he was running. And, when the lab reached him and dropped a shoe at his feet, Dru felt the fear bursting forth inside of him. It was Christy's shoe! Suddenly, Dru knew where Christy was. She had climbed up to the high ledge. She had jumped off. And, she had never come back up.

****

Moriah Sanders stood shaking by the lake shore, tears streaming down her face. Abbi Garcia had her arms around her sister-in-law. She, too, was crying. About 50 feet away, Christopher Sanders was talking with the Hill Valley Sheriff. "How long before the scuba team will be here?" he asked.

"It won't be more than five minutes, sir. I just spoke with them; they're nearly to your house, now."

Chris Sanders went back over to his wife and sister. He told them in a quiet voice, "Sheriff Dresback says the search and rescue truck will be here any minute with a scuba team."

Riah Sanders stepped back from the water and turned to her husband with a sudden change of expression. "Chris, we have to pray! I've felt so devastated by all of this that I forgot about God. He healed Christy when she was so sick with *Shotsie*. God is still with us. And He can save her now…if it's His will."

Chris' shoulders were slumped. He just felt hopeless and weak with sorrow. Looking out at the thin band of lake before him, he thought back to the days when the doctors had said that there was nothing they could do. They had said Christy would die before the night was over. But, at that very moment, even as the doctors were telling them that, their church back in Huron was meeting together for an all-night prayer vigil just for Christy. And, God had heard their prayers. It was from that night that Christy had begun her long road to recovery.

"Riah, Abbi, let's join hands and pray." Chris took hold of his wife's hand and his sister's hand. Standing close to the lake waters, they bowed their heads and prayed for God to work a miracle.

At the end, Moriah added, "Lord, no matter what happens today, I know that you healed Christy when she was so young and sick. Thank you for giving her to us for seven more years. Please, God, save her again—but, not our will, but Yours be done. We pray this in Jesus' name."

When they finished, they saw that two small motorboats were already out on the lake. Two divers were getting ready to plunge into the waters and swim down deep with their bright lights in hopes of recovering Christy's body.

Then, Loopner, who had refused to stay at home, cocked his head and began to whine. Christopher went to give his dog a pat. But the lab ducked away from his hand and ran 20 feet up the shore. Then, he stopped and looked out toward the widening section of the lake. He looked back at his owner, then looked out at the waters and barked. Everyone, even Sheriff Dresback, looked intently out to see what Loopner was barking at. Quite a ways out, coming around the rocky curve, someone was swimming. And, between Loopner's excited barks, they could hear a small voice calling for help.

Suddenly, Loopner stopped waiting for the people to do something. He leaped into the water and started swimming toward the distant figure. The splash of the big dog seemed to wake up the group of people on the shore. With an exclamation of amazement, Sheriff Dresback turned toward the motorboats and started shouting excitedly. He then pointed out toward where Christy was swimming.

Both motorboats immediately went into high gear to reach the little girl before she ran out of strength. The closer boat reached her first and helped her aboard with hearts full of joy and thanksgiving. The second boat pulled Loopner aboard, since he had already swam pretty far out by himself. Loopner thanked his rescuers by soaking them as he shook himself dry, and then by making them deaf with all his ecstatic barking.

Back at the shore, everyone was laughing and crying for joy—even good ol' Sheriff Dresback. The rescue crew checked to make sure Christy wasn't seriously injured in any way, and then drove the Sanders home to give Christy a warm meal and an early bedtime.

****

Later that evening, after Dru had gone to bed, Moriah Sanders stopped into her eldest son's room to say goodnight. Dru was sitting up, looking out toward the lake. "You know what, Mom? When you were all out by Rocky Reach, Uncle Tito got Dad's Bible down from the shelf. He read from Psalm 80—about God coming to save us, you know? Then, he gathered us all around—even the little ones and Baby Lauren—and we prayed." Dru paused and looked back out the window. His mother stayed quiet. So, he added, "Mom, I know God heard us praying and saved Christy. And, for the first time, I know for myself that God really is there and really does hear me pray."

Mrs. Sanders sat down by Dru and looked out the window with him for a minute. Then she looked at her son's face. He was no longer a child—not the baby she had carried or the boy she had taught to ride a horse. He was a young man, ready to make a young man's commitment. "Dru," she said, "you no longer belong to me. You aren't my little boy anymore. You're a man. Now, you belong to God." She kissed her son's forehead and told him, "Tomorrow, you will sit down with your father and his Bible. Dad will read some important verses to you and you will make a man's commitment to God—to the God who is really there, to the God who really does hear you pray."

****

"Your quick thinking saved us from a very risky situation, Master Enoch," Elder Noah Baker said in a kind, but serious tone. Then, he turned to Miriam, "You were right to save the life of the sun-bleached American. It is what is pleasing to the Lord, the Maker of us all—both Edenite and American. However, we were almost discovered before…well, before it was time."

Elder Noah was the oldest of all the Edenites—over ninety—and well respected. Enoch had spoken with him and the other Elders often since he had been chosen to visit the land above the lake. But Miriam had never been so close to him before, nor had she ever visited his home. She felt both nervous and excited. All the most important Edenite meetings were held at Elder Noah's home cavern—for Elder Noah rarely left his home, since his old age now made even a short swim exhausting.

Elder Noah continued, "If we had not sent her out of the old Bethel Entrance Tunnel, the Americans would have surely dived deep into our lake, discovered our lights and fields, and known that we live below them. And," he shook his head, "while we begin to trust the young American strappers, we cannot yet know if we can trust their adults."

A deep-voiced Elder commented, "Sir, when the young blond American tells her parents about us, we will soon know if they can be trusted."

Enoch spoke up in a polite tone. "From all I have heard from Joe, Ana, and Dru, their parents are good people—they do not own slaves, nor do they participate in warring with others. I do not think they would do anything to harm us."

The deep-voiced Elder smiled a bit sadly, and said, "I too trust that they would not *intentionally* try to harm us. However, there is much they could do that could destroy us, even if it were done with innocent intentions."

Eno looked worried, and turned to Elder Noah. "Sir, do you think the Americans would destroy us? They do not seem to be a wicked or warring people."

The Elder looked thoughtfully at Enoch. "Strapper-boy, *wicked* and *warring* are not necessarily paired together. By the grace of God, we Edenites have never fought among ourselves." Then he added, "Our Maker is very wise. He has kept us so busy just trying to survive that we have had no time for such things."

"But," Miriam asked in a very meek voice, "Elder Nathaniel has taught us that war is a cruel and awful thing. Is that not true?"

Elder Noah lifted a bent old hand and thoughtfully scratched a dark old cheek. "Yes, young maiden, war is very cruel, and it is more awful than we can imagine. The father of Elder Matthew Dickens was one of the original scouts. He saw for himself the horrors of war and told them to his son, who in turn told them to me." Elder Noah paused, remembering so many decades ago when he used to sit in his mentor's home cavern to learn the history of the Edenites.

Then, he continued, "War *is* a horrible thing. But, we must not forget that the Holy Book itself is full of wars. Some wars were even started by the command of our Lord God. We cannot always understand His purposes. Greed, hatred, prejudice, malice, and wickedness always have a part in war. However, that does not make everyone who takes part in a war greedy and wicked. It must be hard for you young ones to understand, but we should never be too quick to judge. And, we must always look to the Holy Bible for our answers."

Enoch and Miriam both nodded solemnly, though they only partly understood what he was saying.

"Well," Elder Noah said with a note of humor in his voice, "it has turned out that God has chosen an unexpected ambassador to our people—a tiny little white-haired American maiden. We will trust that God our Maker gives her the right words to introduce us to her parents. And," he added with a serious tone, "to hide us from the Americans who might seek to destroy us. It is time we discussed this possibility and come to some decisions."

On hearing the start of this new topic, a third Elder said, "Elder Noah, it is time we send the strappers to work in the fields. They are quite short-handed, since we have four new cases of the *Shotsie* reported this week—including my grandson, James." The man shook his head and added, "We must ask God for mercy."

As Enoch and Miriam slid into the waters to leave Elder Noah's home, they heard James' grandfather add, "I am afraid he has it in the worst way. There is very little hope for him."

****

Dozens of marshmallows pelted Billy as he finished up another 'chapter' of his story. Catching one marshmallow in mid-air, he popped it in his mouth and said, "I'll tell you more tomorrow. For now, finish up your snack and get ready for bed. It's past nine o'clock."

While the other boys ran toward the *guys'* side of camp to get ready for bed, Todd caught up with Aaron. "Hey, Aaron? Can I ask you something?"

Aaron felt a little uncomfortable after the way Todd had treated him at school, but tried to *forgive and forget*. "Uh, sure," he said in a friendly tone.

"Well…um…first I want to say I'm sorry I acted so dumb." Todd stood still and hung his head.

Aaron shrugged his shoulders and said, "Hey, man, it's okay." Then, he added with a half-smile, "I guess I'm kinda like Joe showing up in the middle of Hill Valley…"

"Yeah…" Todd smiled. But, then he looked down again. "I guess that makes me like Brent and Trent—the super jerks."

"Naw," Aaron said. "I mean…anyway…don't worry. Now, what did you want to ask me?"

Todd walked beside Aaron for a minute, then said, "My uncle—Tony—is black. I haven't really ever said much to him, though I've gone to visit my aunt and their kids with my mom. Anyway, now I kinda want him to know…well, I guess I want him to know that I'm glad he's my uncle. What do you think I should do?"

Aaron was thoughtful for a bit, then asked, "Is Tony a Christian?"

Todd answered, "Yes—like way! He sings in the church choir and everything."

Aaron laughed. "I don't know if singing in the choir makes someone a Christian. But, if he *is* a Christian, then that makes your job much easier." Aaron stopped outside the boys' camp area to finish. "If he really is a Christian, then I'll bet he's been praying for you all along. In that case, you can just tell him what you told me. Say, 'I'm sorry, man. I'm glad you're my uncle.'"

"But," Todd asked, "like, what if he's mad at me and tells me to get lost?"

Aaron shook his head. "I don't think he will. But, if he does, you can understand why he would. So, just give him some time and keep on treating him with respect."

Then, Aaron shook off the serious conversation by giving Todd a hard shove and calling, "I'll race you to the outhouse." And off they ran.

CHAPTER 9

Rosa, Beauty, and Paco frisked happily through the meadows around the Garcias' property. Dru, on Azúl, watched as Christy urged little Beauty over toward the slender section of the lake. The day after her near drowning, Christy had spent nearly two hours talking in private with her parents. Soon afterwards, Dru's parents had gone to talk with Uncle Tito and Aunt Abbi. Then, today, his dad and Uncle Tito had taken the day off and were locked out on the back patio in serious conversation. Dru wondered what Christy had told his parents.

Suddenly, Christy yelled out, "Look, Dru! Do you see over on the ledge? It must be Enoch. And it looks like he has Miriam with him!"

Dru, Joe, and Ana pulled up next to Christy and looked over toward Rocky Reach. Up on the high ledge, they all saw Eno's tall figure waving to them. They also saw a girl. She was as tall as Enoch, but dark-skinned. "Who on earth is Miriam?" Dru asked.

Ana answered, "I remember Eno once told us that Miriam was his best friend. But, I've never seen her anywhere near Hill Valley. She looks black...and I would have been the first one to welcome her to town if I had seen her."

Joe turned to Christy with a surprised look. "How do you know that's Miriam?"

Christy looked a bit embarrassed. Then said, "Hey, it looks like they really want us to come over. We'd better go. It might be important." And she encouraged Beauty to get moving toward Rocky Reach.

By the time the horses had reached the small group of trees close to the lake, Enoch and Miriam had climbed down from the ledge and ran over to meet them. "We are so glad that you came here today," Enoch said. "We prayed you would. It is so important that we talk with you." Then, seeing the others looking at Miriam, he added, "This is my best friend. She is Miriam, the daughter of Mr. Gideon BearClaw."

Christy went forward and hugged Miriam. "Miriam is the one who saved my life when I was dumb enough to jump off the high ledge by myself." Everyone laughed a bit at seeing how much taller Miriam was than Christy. With the one being so blond and the other dark—they certainly were two very different girls.

"Actually," Miriam said, "I also had the help of another strapper—James. He is the reason we hoped you would come to the lake today. Doctor Daniel and Doctor Sarah have both tried everything. They think he will die."

"But," Enoch broke in, "Miriam and I thought and prayed and talked as much as we were able while working in the fields this morning, and we came up with a plan. We feel sure that you Americans must have something that will save James."

Ana said eagerly, "Our mom's a nurse. She works two days a week at the hospital. I'll bet she could help." Then, she asked curiously, "Where *do* you and your friends live? Is it far from here?"

Enoch and Miriam looked at Christy. Ana, Dru, and Joe looked at Christy. "Well," Christy said awkwardly, "ummm…it's not far at all. Actually, it's just right down there," she said pointing into the water.

Dru pulled his eyebrows together, then took a step backwards in disbelief. "Like, are you saying they, like, live underwater?"

"Yeah, I guess…kinda." Christy giggled at her brother's expression.

Then, Dru, Ana, and Joe all turned to look questioningly at Enoch and Miriam. Eno smiled a bit nervously and answered, "Uh, that's right."

"Wow!" Dru said. "Then, you really are alien-fish-people?"

Ana woke up from her amazement and gave Dru a swat on the arm. "No way! Do they leave a trail of slime? No. Can they breathe underwater? Ummm…I don't think so. They must be people just like we are." Then, she turned to Miriam and asked, "So, you can't breathe underwater, can you?"

Miriam explained, "Actually, we really live in the air-filled caverns that spread out under the land across this part of the lake. Our fathers began living in the caverns long ago, when slavery, hatred, and war filled your land under the sun." After a pause, she continued, "But, Enoch says that there is no more slavery or war in Hill Valley. Is that true?"

Joe spoke up for the first time. "It's true there's no war here—nowhere near us. And, slavery has been illegal for a long time. But, that doesn't mean everything is perfect…" Joe couldn't help thinking about just a few days before when Brent had purposely knocked him into a mud puddle and then acted as if it had been an accident. Out loud, he just sighed. There might not be any more slavery in America, but life in Hill Valley wasn't always easy if your skin was dark.

Enoch stepped forward. "Please," he said earnestly, "I do not know how much time we have. Is it possible for us to talk to your mother?"

With Miriam behind Ana on Rosa and Enoch behind Dru on Azúl, the friends galloped toward the Garcias' home.

****

That night, a group of four dark men sat waiting behind the large rocks along the shores of Rocky Reach. They were all strong and very tall—closer to seven foot, than six. Still, when they heard footsteps approaching their hiding place, they looked at each other nervously. They had never met adult Americans before. Could they be trusted? History lessons of the Americans' strange and often cruel way of life made them wonder if they had made the right choice in accepting their help. But then, one of the Edenites stepped forward ahead of the others and came out into the open.

Tomás and Abbi Garcia both stopped when they saw the giant in front of them. Enoch had told them that their guides would be tall. But, hearing *tall* and seeing *tall* are two different things. After all, Tito himself was only five foot, six inches tall.

Mustering his courage, Tito stepped forward. "Hello, my friend. I am Tomás Garcia. And, this is my wife, Abigail. We have come to see if we can help those of your people who are sick."

Mr. Gideon BearClaw extended his hand to shake Tito's hand. "I am the father of Miriam—Gideon BearClaw." Then, turning to the man next to him, he said, "This is the father of James—Mr. Seth Smith. We are grateful for your kind desire to help. Let us go quickly, before we are seen."

Tito and Abbi had been told what to expect. So, Tito walked right over to the edge of the lake as a sign of good faith. Abbi, however, was afraid and hesitated. The three men behind her hesitated as well. Abbi would have been shocked if she had known that these three powerful men were just as nervous and uncertain as she was. Seeing the men waiting for her, she ran to catch up with her husband. Once they were both in the water, Tito kissed his wife and whispered, "Don't be afraid. God is with us."

Then, Mr. Gideon and the others slid in beside them. Two men took hold of Tito, and two took hold of Abbi. Mr. Gideon warned, "Hold your breath." Then, the strong Edenites pulled the Garcias underwater. Gripping them tightly by the arms, the men pulled them quickly down. Tito marveled as the dark waters began to brighten as they went down. Abbi simply kept her eyes shut tight and prayed. But, sooner than she had expected, she found herself surfacing inside a lighted cave. And, just as Christy had told her, a few sleepy birds fluttered close to the cave walls.

Mr. Seth told them, "This is but the East Entrance Cavern. It is quite a few more swims before we reach my home. Many of the tunnels will be dark. You must trust us. Are you ready?"

Abbi looked at the men holding her up in the water. She felt a God-given peace, and all her fear seemed to melt away. She smiled and said, "I think you must be angels in disguise—there's no other way I can believe this is really happening."

The man on her left laughed out loud. "How did you know that my name is Gabriel?" Then, with lightened spirits, they all began their journey toward the Seth-Smith home cavern.

****

Billy finished up and was about to dismiss the kids to their next activity. But, suddenly, a loud shout came from up in the tree he'd been leaning against. A large net fell down, landing on Billy and knocking off his ever-present baseball cap. And, before he had time to even try to roll out from under the net, four boys and three girls had the net secured around him.

Darin jumped down out of the tree and told the rest of the kids, "Billy is super-spectacu-splendiferously ticklish. I'm sure a minute or two of tickle-torture will make him *beg us to let him* tell some more of the story."

But, before anyone could start tickling, Billy put up his hands in surrender, "Okay, okay. I'll tell a little more," he laughed. Then, he turned to Darin as they unwrapped him and promised, "You'll pay for this, traitor."

Darin just smiled smugly and sat down with the others to hear the story.

****

Back at home, Joe looked toward the distant tree-covered hills and wished he were already there. He just felt like he needed to be alone. So much had happened in the last six months of his life—it was almost more than he could digest. Uncle Chris had seemed to know how Joe was feeling that evening, for he had told him, "Hey, Joe, since I'm here with all the kids while your parents are away, why don't you go for a night ride with Paco?"

Tapping Paco's sides with his heels, Joe felt the surge of freedom that always came when he was atop his galloping pony. It was as if he could outrun everything—the loneliness he felt for the friends he'd left in Huron, the unkind remarks some of the boys made about his color, and now, the fears he faced as his parents disappeared into an unknown underwater world.

Joe ran Paco until he felt he should give him a rest. After walking him for a few minutes, Joe slid off his pony and took him by the bridle. Together, they stopped and looked into the deep woods they had been riding toward. Now that he was here, Joe wasn't so sure about going into the dark woods. Paco, however, could sense the cool brook that was within and stamped impatiently to go forward. So, Joe remounted Paco and told him, "Go ahead, boy. You lead."

After a few minutes, Paco splashed into a wide but shallow creek bed and paused for a long drink. Joe dismounted and listened to the woodsy night sounds. Now that he was all alone, he felt he could really talk to God. So, while his pony wandered here and there, Joe told God how he had been feeling. And he asked God to help him act and react in the right way. Then, he prayed for his parents and for Enoch's sick friend. Finally, Joe felt completely peaceful. He went to fetch Paco to start back toward home.

Nearing the edge of the woods, Paco paused and turned his nose and ears back in the direction of the brook. Suddenly, the hairs prickled on the back of Joe's neck. Some sort of animal was calling—it was a raspy, hoarse kind of yell. Was it a bear, or maybe a cougar? Joe was ready to race Paco home. But, Paco didn't take his lead. Instead, the horse turned toward the sound and nickered softly.

Joe leaned toward his horse's ear and whispered, "Chico loco! Come on. Let's get out of here!" Then, he pulled Paco's reins to turn him back toward the fields. Paco turned, but took two steps backwards instead of forwards.

Then, again, the raspy call floated toward them on the night air. This time, Joe heard it more clearly. He realized that it wasn't an animal's call, but a person calling for help. Now, turning Paco toward the sound, he relaxed his hold on the reins and said, "Go on, boy! Let's go find him!"

****

The twelve leaders from the three cities of Eden were gathered at the Sunshine Caverns for an emergency meeting. Even old Elder Noah had allowed himself to be pulled to the meeting in a breathe-easy bag (something he despised). Everyone had had time to discuss the situation. Now, different people were offering their opinions.

One Elder from Bethlehem spoke up. "My wife had the *Shotsie* when she was young, Mrs. Abigail. I do not understand why you cannot use her blood to heal James. I would think Edenite blood for an Edenite would be better than American blood for an Edenite." Several Elders murmured in agreement.

Then, a tall, dark Elder said hesitantly, "I myself have had the *Shotsie*. I am both male and look similar to James. Perhaps my blood would be better for the strapper." Most of the Elders nodded their heads. It seemed very logical.

Elder Noah looked toward the Garcias and said, "Mrs. Abigail, is there any reason Elder Silas cannot give his blood for James?"

"Sir," Abbi answered, "it is very likely that many of the Edenites have blood that could help James. The question is, which ones?" She took a breath and continued, "Up in…in *America*, we have been using other people's blood to help the sick for many, many years. And, we have learned a lot of things. One thing we have found is that there are several different kinds of blood types. Many people share a common blood type, though some are rarer than others. However, you must be careful, because you cannot mix blood of different types—it will only make the sick person worse, not better."

"Well," Elder Noah said, "it would seem that Elder Silas should have the same blood type. Or, perhaps, Mr. Joseph. He is also both male and carries many of the physical features that James carries—tight curls, very dark, wide mouth and nose. And he lives in Bethel, does he not?"

"Excuse me, sir," Tito spoke up, "I can see how you might think that the more people look alike, the more likely they are to have the same blood type. But, it really doesn't seem to work that way. Looks, skin color, even if you are male or female, none of these guarantee a blood type." He went on, "Now, Abbi brought two blood type test strips in her medical kit. She used one to find out what James' blood type is. She has one more. She can test Elder Silas or Mr. Joseph. However, it's much more likely that either James' mother or father would share his blood type—no matter what they look like. Have either of them had *Shotsie*?"

Dr. Sarah spoke up, "No. Nor have any of his sisters."

"Then," Abbi said, "I am willing to test anyone you suggest. But, if it is not a match, it will take me hours to get more tests, and maybe hours more to find a match among your people. That is why I am suggesting we use Christy's blood. I know her blood matches James'. She has had *Shotsie*, and survived. Her blood will help James. And," she continued, "the sooner we decide, the better. James is very sick. If we wait too long, nothing will help him."

"But," an Elder questioned, "how can you be certain the blood of your daughter will not harm James? I mean, she is...well, an American. And, she is everything James is not—female, white, blond, and extremely short. It seems impossible."

Another Elder added, "I am just not sure we are meant to mix American and Edenite blood. Can it be pleasing to God?"

Mrs. Bethany spoke up, "Come now! Is it not God who has given us the possibility of saving James? In the past, our good doctors did all they could. But, still, many of our people died of various troubles. When they died, we were grieved, though we trusted in the love of God. Will we now reject the only means of healing James, just because it comes in the form of a sun-bleached American maiden?"

Another very old Elder from Bethsaida spoke up, "You all seem to have forgotten that we ourselves are descended from Americans. Many of us here have the blood of the Dickens brothers inside of us. And we know that they were blond and white—perhaps as white as Miss Christy."

"Does Master James have Dickens blood in him?" Dr. Daniel asked.

"It should make little difference," James' grandfather spoke up. "For the Holy Bible says that we all came from two people—Adam and Eve, and even Eve was made from a part of Adam." He looked at the people around him. "So, what color were Adam and Eve? As a black man, I have always assumed they were black. However, it is my guess that Mrs. Abigail, here, has always assumed that they were white." He continued, "It is obvious that over time, the two original people produced many children with many different appearances. And, from those children came all people—a vast and amazing variety, even just among our mostly tall, dark Edenites. I can hardly imagine what it must be like among all the people that cover the world."

Tomás spoke up, "It's almost beyond belief. But, you're right—all that diversity goes back to two people. So, in the end, we all share the same father and mother. And, so, we all really belong to the same family."

Elder Noah replied, "I agree." Then, turning to all the people gathered, he said, "I do not fully understand all the mysteries Mrs. Abigail has tried to explain about blood types and how the blood of one person can heal another. But, I do know that it was the leading of the Maker that caused Master Enoch to go up to America. And, it is God that has brought us to this point."

With a sigh he continued, "We have little time. The good doctors have said that we will lose Master James without a miracle of God." He paused, then continued, "I believe Mrs. Abigail and her daughter are the miracle the Creator has given us. I vote that we bring Miss Christy down to share her blood with James."

An Elder from each of the three cities of Eden stood up to pray for God's wisdom. Then, an informal hand vote decided unanimously that Mrs. Abigail should return with six strong guides to bring Mr. Christopher and Christy down to James, along with the needed medical supplies. Mr. Tomás would stay behind to answer the Edenites' many questions.

****

At the end of this part of the story, Jill asked Billy, "Is what Mrs. Abbi said for real, really true? I mean, could I give my blood to save Tasha, even though she's black and way taller than me and all?"

Billy smiled and said, "Well, you do have to consider if you and Tasha have the same blood type. But, if you do, then you could give your blood to help her."

Here, Abel jumped up. "And, like, listen to this! This is a *for real, really true* story. Back during the Vietnam War, there were two men in the same group of army engineers, called *tunnel rats*—totally cool name, don't you think? Well, anyway, though they had the same job, they were way different. One of the men was totally white, with blond hair and all. Get this, he was so white, his nickname was *Snow*. Well, the other man was black. He was so black that his friends said that he was blacker than the ace of spades. But, even though they were as different as can be as far as skin color goes, they were *for real, really true* friends.

"Anyway, a long time later, the black man got really sick. He had severe diabetes and needed a new kidney, or he would die. Now—here's the key—the new kidney had to be a very close tissue match. Lots of people were tested to see if their kidney was a good match. Now, you would expect a family member to have the best match. But, nope, it didn't turn out that way. Now, guess—just guess—who had the only good match? *That's right!* Incredible as it seems, it was Snow who had the best tissue match for his dark-skinned friend. And, he donated one of his kidneys to save his life.

"So, there! You see, we for real, really, and truly are *one blood.* Some people have dark skin, some have light, but there's only one race. We're all part of the same race—the *human race!"*

CHAPTER 10

Around trees, under branches, through the underbrush, Paco carried Joe through the dark woods toward the voice calling for help. Then, up ahead, Joe saw a large shape swaying back and forth. It seemed to be floating in mid-air. And it was groaning—a miserable, pitiful sound. Again, the hairs on Joe's neck stood up. His legs said *turn around and run!* But Paco's legs didn't seem to be getting the same message, and the horse kept moving toward the dark, eerie shape.

By the time the boy and his horse were within 20 feet of the...the whatever it was...Joe began to realize that something about it wasn't right. Bending himself over to the side, he took a new look at the shape in front of him and saw that it was indeed a person. However, the person was hanging upside down by one foot. What on earth!

"Sir," Joe called out to the upside down figure. "What's happened? I'm here to help."

The dangling shape suddenly jumped to life, flailing and shouting in a boy's hoarse voice, "Help me! I'm gonna die! Please help me!" Then, the voice said, "Wait! Watch out! There's a big ditch right under me. Don't come too close."

Joe had dismounted Paco and was walking toward the boy when he heard the warning. Stopping in his tracks, Joe searched the ground carefully. Sure enough, about four feet in front of him was the edge of a large hole. Following the circle around, Joe realized that this was a *very* large hole, and the boy was hanging from a rope right above the center of it.

"Whoa, man!" Joe called. "You got yourself caught in one major bear trap or somethin'. It's gonna be tough getting you down."

The boy groaned. And, in his raspy voice, he explained, "That's just what it was supposed to be—a bear trap. If I hadn't dropped my knife, I coulda cut myself down. I feel like I've been here for hours. I think I'm gonna die…"

Climbing down into the ditch, Joe stood under the boy. He looked up and the boy looked down. Then, they both jerked with recognition. Joe took a step back. It was Brent! He couldn't believe it. The boy who, along with his cousin, had made it his goal in life to make Joe feel unwelcome in Hill Valley. Of all the boys in the world, the last one Joe would want to rescue was Brent.

Brent must have known what Joe was thinking, because he started crying, "I'm gonna die…I know I'm gonna die."

Joe pulled himself together and pushed aside all feelings of anger and the temptation for revenge. He remembered the peace that God had given him back by the brook. Then, looking back up at Brent, he found he had forgiven him. Just like that. When he resisted the urge to hate and set his heart on God, then he was able to forgive.

"Listen, Brent," Joe said in a calm tone. "I'm not going to leave you here. I have a rope that I could toss to you. But, I'm not sure if that will help. Do you have any ideas?"

Brent answered in a relieved voice, "Thanks, man! If you can find my knife, you could cut me down. I can't pull myself up anymore. I've tried till I'm worn out. But, if you climb up that tree and scoot out on that branch, you could cut it."

Joe thought that through. Then, looking at the branch, he said, "I have my own knife. Problem is, I don't think that branch will hold both your weight and mine."

Brent dangled silently for a minute. Then, he kind of laughed. "Guess I hadn't thought of that. It sure wouldn't have held a bear, then, would it?"

"The other problem," Joe continued, "is that even if I could cut your rope, you would fall head first into this big ol' ditch. That doesn't sound like a good idea." After a pause, he said, "Maybe I should go for help."

"No! No, please, no!" Brent begged. "I've been hanging here too long already. I feel like my head's gonna explode. I'm gonna barf, man. My leg's gonna fall off. Don't go. If you go, I'm gonna die!"

"Okay, man," Joe tried to calm him down. "I won't go unless I really have to. But, stay quiet for a minute, I have to try to think."

Brent tried to stay quiet, but couldn't help groaning occasionally.

"Brent, I have an idea," Joe said excitedly. "I'm gonna take my rope and climb to that bigger branch kinda above the one you're tied on. Then, I'll lower my rope to you. You tie it around yourself real secure. Then, I'll pull you up. I don't know if I can get you all the way up. But, at least that way you'll be upright, and all your weight won't be on your one ankle."

"Do it, man!" Brent said. "Hurry!"

Joe grabbed his rope from Paco and started to climb. It wasn't as easy as he had thought. But, he made it to the higher branch and crawled himself part way out. But, halfway there, he was stuck—it was too thin to go any farther out.

"Good grief," he called to Brent. "How in the world did you get out on that skinny branch to tie on your rope?"

"You need to hang upside down," Brent explained. "Cross your knees over the top of the branch, and go hand over hand."

"You mean you do that kind of thing just for fun?" Joe asked.

"All the time," Brent responded.

"Okay, here goes nothing!" Joe said, letting himself fall into a sloth-like position. It was pretty scary. Joe's respect for Brent had to go up a few notches. Once he was in the right place, Joe wrapped one part of his rope around the tree branch. Then he tossed the long end down toward Brent.

After five failed tries, Joe started to panic. Now that he was hanging upside down, he began to feel dizzy. His arms and legs were tired, and it was a long fall down. Slowly pulling the loose rope back up to get it ready for another toss, he called down to Brent, "Man, you'd better start praying. God knows where you're at better than I do. He's gonna have to be the one to get this rope to you."

Brent didn't say anything, but he caught the next toss and tied it securely around his chest. Then, he took hold of the hanging rope in both hands. "Please, Joe, pull me up." It was the first time Brent had ever called Joe by his real name.

Joe had gotten himself back upright on his branch and got near the base of the tree where he felt more stable. Then, he pulled with all his might. It turned out that he could only pull if Brent hopped up a bit. So, with each little hop, Joe would pull the rope tighter until Brent was high enough to use the rope that his foot was stuck in as leverage. Then, with Brent pushing up against the bear-trap rope, Joe kept shortening *his* rope until Brent was nearly upright, hanging from Joe's rope around his chest. And, from there, Brent reached up and grabbed hold of the tree branch that the bear snare had been tied to and wrapped his legs around it.

After a bit of a rest, Brent crawled himself to the trunk of the tree, and then down to the ground. Joe climbed down after him. Both collapsed in exhaustion under the tree.

Finally, Joe said, "If you can get onto Paco, I'll lead you to a brook for a drink. Then, I'll get you home."

Before mounting Paco, Brent turned to Joe. "Hey, man," he said in an embarrassed tone. "I'm real sorry I've been such a big jerk. I don't know why I was. But, I won't do any of that no more."

Joe was embarrassed, too. "I guess it's okay. I guess dark skin is kinda different here in Hill Valley. But, now you know I'm just like anyone else. So, let's be friends."

"You bet!" Brent said with a smile.

After getting a drink, Brent climbed back onto Paco. "If your horse ain't too scared, my four-wheeler's just about five minutes from here. We can ride that with him following. But, I'll need your help. I don't think I can drive it. My head still ain't right."

"Totally cool!" Joe said excitedly. "Like, I've always wanted to drive a four-wheeler!"

****

Holding to the rope that was tied around the waist of her guide, Christy let herself be pulled through yet another black underwater tunnel. On her last visit to Eden, Christy had felt curious and amazed. But now, she felt scared and uncertain.

Christy's father and mother had woken her out of a deep sleep and urged her to dress quickly. Then, Aunt Abbi had explained that they needed her blood to cure James.

"My blood?" Christy had asked, suddenly wide-awake. Aunt Abbi had calmly assured her that it wouldn't hurt much, and that she would still have plenty of blood left for herself.

But Christy wasn't feeling so calm. She didn't like needles. She didn't like to see or even talk about blood. Come to think of it, she didn't even like James. He had gone out of his way to make it plain that he didn't like her or trust her. It seemed ridiculous to her that he would hate her just because she was white. It was the first time that Christy had felt the sting of prejudice. It was just…well, totally unfair. She couldn't help it that she wasn't tall and black, could she?

Coming up into the *Welcome Mat* before the Seth-Smith family cavern, Christy's guides waited for Mr. Christopher and Mrs. Abbi, along with their guides, to catch up. Then, they rang the entry bell. Immediately, it was answered with the deeper *welcome* bell. Christy caught her breath and dived down with her guides into the Smith's parlor room. James' mother was there to meet them.

"Thank the Maker you have come," Mrs. Hannah Smith said with relief in her voice. But she couldn't help staring at Christy and Abbi as they climbed out of the water. "My," she said hesitantly, "James was right. You Americans certainly are…uh…different." Then, she added nervously, "Mr. Amos, are you sure this is the right thing to do?"

Her father-in-law took hold of her hand, "Hannah, dear, do not be afraid. These tiny, sun-bleached Americans look different from what we are used to, but it is only color and size. On the inside, we are all basically the same." Then, he pointed to two cats that had come out from the plants in hopes of getting a treat. "Look at Tango and Pan-pan. One is fluffy, the other smooth. One is striped, the other patched. One is bigger, the other smaller. Yet, they are both still cats. And, their kittens are an interesting mix of the two. God made it so that people can have the same diversity, and still be people."

Mrs. Hannah seemed to accept what Mr. Amos had said, and she turned to welcome the Americans to her home.

"Please, forgive my fears…it is just that I have heard so many strange things about Americans. James is right back here in the guest room."

****

Sometime later, James Smith opened his eyes. The light in the room seemed painful to him. Groaning, he turned his head—looking for his mother. Instead, he saw beside him a strange white-skinned lady. She was wearing light-colored clothes and had light-colored hair. And, she was smiling at him. "She must be an angel," James thought to himself. He had seen several pictures of angels in the Dickens Brother's books. This lady resembled them in many ways.

Looking around the room, he thought to himself, "If she is an angel, then, I must have died. Dr. Sarah said I would probably die. And, Dr. Daniel said that I must prepare my heart to meet the Savior." Fear suddenly overwhelmed his heart. He had not paid any attention to Dr. Daniel's words. He had felt so confident that he was too strong to die. Now, he was dead, and what would Jesus say about the life he had lived?

Suddenly, it all came crashing down on him—his unkind words to Enoch, his pride in being so big and dark and that his grandfather was an Elder, his jealousy of his mother's affection for his little sisters, and his hatred toward the little American girl. These all stood in front of him and condemned him. He was not ready. He had not put his trust in the Savior. He had not asked for forgiveness. Now, it was too late. Sorrow and fear overwhelmed him, and the tears began running down his cheeks. "I am sorry, I am so sorry. I was wrong. I am so sorry," he sobbed out loud.

But then, his mother—his own dear mother—was leaning close to his face. "James, James," she called gently. "Do not cry, my darling. I am here. Everything is okay. You are going to be okay."

James took hold of his mother's hand and looked into her face. Then he turned to look around him. His father was close to his side and reached out to take hold of his other hand. "Where am I?" James asked in confusion.

"Oh, dear James," his mother said, "you are back in your own room. When we saw that you were getting stronger, we moved you out of the guest room."

"Oh," was all James could think of to say. But then he added, "Why did I not die?"

His grandfather had come into the room and answered, "Because God sent a little angel to save your life, that is why."

James looked at the smiling white lady. "Is she the angel?" he asked.

"Well," his mother answered, "she is an angel for sure. But, I think your grandfather was referring to little Miss Christy."

"Miss Christy?" James asked. "*Christy?* You mean that little sun-bleached American? How could she save me? I thought I saved her."

Mrs. Abbi replied, "You did, James. And her parents are so very grateful. However, this time, Christy saved you—by giving some of her blood to you. She was the only one we knew of whose blood could cure you."

"Oh," James said again. Then he closed his eyes and said, "I never thought a tiny little sun-bleached maiden could save *me*."

"Well, James," his father replied, "you know it is really God who saved you. He just used Miss Christy to do it." Then, he continued, "And I think He was very wise in doing so. I am afraid that our family has had a bad seed of pride growing up in it. The Creator has made it clear that He is just as pleased to use a white American as He is to use a black Edenite. For, it is true that we can *all* trace our family tree back through history to Adam and Eve."

James sighed. “I feel very tired, but I am not afraid anymore.” Then, just before falling back to sleep, James asked, “Grandpa, when I get better, can I go up to America and thank Miss Christy for saving my life?”

****

“The End,” Billy said.

“Wait a minute,” David complained. “What happened when James got better and went up to America?”

“Yeah,” Aaron joined in. “And, like, what did all the people think when they saw all the seven-foot tall Edenites?”

“And…” Jill started to ask…

“Whoa, whoa!” Billy said holding up his hands. “I’m leaving the rest for you all to fill in with your own imaginations.”

“Man!” Jack said as he jumped up, “I’ll bet James joins a swim team and sets a new world record.”

“Yeah,” Jill laughed as they headed off toward the fields. “And, I’ll bet that Miriam goes to college and becomes the world’s greatest doctor for the Edenites.”

David smiled as they climbed the fence to get their horses. “I think Hill Valley and the Edenites should set up an exchange student program.”

As everyone bustled around to get to the horse they’d ridden the day before, Aaron paused and turned around. Seeing Todd still outside the fence—alone—he called, “Hurry up, Todd, the four of us boys can make up a team.”

With a giant smile, Todd raced forward to join his new friends.

Seeing the boys running together, Billy lifted his eyes to Heaven and said, “Thank you, God!”

A NOTE FROM DAVID

Hola Hermanos!

This is David Avila. As you know, I'm Latino—and I really do 'look the part.' I have black hair, dark eyes, dark skin, and, yes, I'm kinda short. Sometimes, people really do treat me differently just because of the way I look. But my parents have helped me forgive and keep an open heart.

Then, last year, God gave me a different perspective. There was a boy in our church with pretty serious cerebral palsy. He's partially paralyzed and even has trouble talking. Anyway, one day, my dad sat me down and told me he was disappointed in the way I was so obviously avoiding Jimmy.

I was shocked to realize that I was treating Jimmy just like I didn't want people to treat me. So, I asked God to help me to show Jimmy respect and kindness. And, you know what? I found out he loves baseball. I finally found someone who follows all the Major League stats and actually understands what I'm talking about.

Paz!
David

ABOUT THE AUTHORS

John is a nationally certified middle school teacher. He has worked with teenagers for the past 20 years, both as a teacher and as a youth pastor. Lisa received her college degree in English Literature. She has also been active working with youth for the past 20 years. The Foxes live on a ten-acre farm in Central Ohio where they homeschool their six children. They also own lots of dogs and a variety of fun farm animals.

Authors' Note

Although this book is a work of fiction, the science discussed regarding the origin of 'races' is *real* and is based on the Bible. Different genetic studies have shown that the *Adam and Eve theory* is scientifically sound. These studies show that it is genetically feasible that the wide variety of people groups we see today could possibly be traced back to two original people. This would mean that there are no 'different races.' We are all one race—the human race, created by God in His own image.

As always, we encourage our readers to ask questions and to do further research.

RECOMMENDED RESOURCES:

ONE HUMAN FAMILY

A fascinating and deeply informative read that goes way beyond the normal 'all one race' conclusion. Combines sensitivity with a rejection of 'political correctness'. This blow-by-blow tour of race-related issues across the world is unlike any other creation book you've ever read. For many, it will make 'the lights go on'—not just about race but the whole biblical 'big picture' of human history.

CREATION NOT CONFUSION DVD

In these fast-paced and informative presentations, Gary Bates demonstrates with stunning clarity how beliefs about where we came from determine our overall worldview, our behavior, and where we think we go when we die—and why the church should embrace this issue if it is to be the force it once was when engaging the culture.

REFUTING EVOLUTION 2

This sequel comprehensively refutes arguments used to support evolution (as presented in TV documentaries and *Scientific American*). Read leading evolutionists in their own words, and then find straightforward answers from science and the Bible. *Refuting Evolution 2* will prepare you to answer the best arguments thrown at you by peers, teachers, neighbors, and skeptics.

THE STRANGER ON THE ROAD TO EMMAUS

Many people today have 'little pieces of theology' and outside 'facts' through which they interpret the Bible. This book explains the greatest Bible themes clearly and logically by chronologically binding the entire text into one great universal drama.

GOD: THE MASTER DESIGNER DVD

Darwin was totally unaware of the amazing machinery in even supposedly simple cells, which is essential for life to exist. And even larger-scale designs are outside the reach of the alleged mutation plus selection mechanisms of evolution. Dr Jonathan Sarfati demonstrates fantastic and compelling evidence of design—so advanced that human engineers are learning and copying from it.

WHO MADE GOD? DVD

The question "If God created the universe, then who created God?" is often used to challenge the truth of the Genesis account of creation. Learn how to respond, and see how the universe displays all the hallmarks of complex and purposeful design. Indeed the "heavens declare the Glory of God" and reveal His purpose for mankind.

CREATION.com

For more information on creation/evolution and Bible-science issues

---

AUSTRALIA
Creation Ministries International (Australia)
PO Box 4545
Eight Mile Plains, QLD 4113

Phone: (07) 3340 9888
Fax: (07) 3340 9889
ABN 31 010 120 304

CANADA
Creation Ministries International (Canada)
300 Mill St, Unit 7
Kitchener, ON N2M 5G8

Phone: (519) 746–7616
Orders & donations: 1-888-251-5360
Fax: (519) 746–7617

NEW ZEALAND
Creation Ministries International (NZ)
PO Box 39005
Howick, Auckland 2145

Phone/Fax: (09) 537 4818
A Registered Charitable Trust

SINGAPORE
Creation Ministries International (Singapore)
Clementi Central Post Office
PO Box 195
Singapore 911207

Phone: 9698 4292

SOUTH AFRICA
Creation Ministries International (SA)
PO Box 3349
Durbanville 7551

Phone: (021) 979 0107
Fax: (086) 519 0555

UK & Europe
Creation Ministries International (UK/Europe)
15 Station St,
Whetstone, Leicestershire, LE8 6JS

Phone: 0116-2848-999

USA
Creation Ministries International (USA)
PO Box 350,
Powder Springs, GA 30127

Phone: (800) 616-1264
Fax: (770) 439-9784

OTHER COUNTRIES
Creation Ministries International
PO Box 4545
Eight Mile Plains,
QLD 4113, Australia

Phone: +617 3340 9888
Fax: +617 3340 9889